Now, Please

Other Titles by Willow Summers

Jessica Brodie Diaries

Back in the Saddle, Book 1

Hanging On, Book 2

A Wild Ride, Book 3

Growing Pains Series

Lost and Found, Book 1

Overcoming Fear, Book 2

Butterflies in Honey, Book 3

Growing Pains Boxed Set (books 1–3)

Love and Chaos, Cassie's Story

Surviving Love, a novel

Now, Please

By Willow Summers

Chapter 1

I WALKED INTO Hunter Carlisle's office on Monday morning as a sexual equal. I was flying by the seat of my pants, not regulated by a personal contract. Hunter was trusting me. More importantly, he had allowed himself to open up just a crack and let me wiggle in. It was a huge milestone in his life and I was grabbing it by the horns and hanging on.

He was sitting at his desk with the soft light of the morning spilling over his broad shoulders. My breath caught in my throat for just a moment before tingling overcame my body.

The man was gorgeous, and I thanked God that he had come to his senses. Otherwise I'd have to start stalking him. I still might, just for the thrill.

"Hey," I said, putting his coffee on the corner of the desk just as I had every working day for the last month. He glanced up at my voice. His hooded, smoldering eyes reminding me of twisted sheets and writhing bodies. I gulped, a little too loudly. "Uh, I have some things to go over concerning my salary…when you're ready."

He glanced at the clock at the top of his desk before leaning back. "You know my schedule—when do I have time?"

"Now, or at the end of the day. That's pretty much it."

Hunter clasped his hands in his lap as he studied me. His gaze slid down my body before nodding. "I have other plans for you this evening. Sit."

My stomach flip-flopped. The expectation of what he had planned gave me a hot flash. I sat gingerly and tried to ignore the pounding in my core. I handed over my folder.

Hunter took it without a word, opened it, and glanced at the contents. He laid the folder on his desk. "I know what kind of work you do, Olivia. What kind of figures do you have in mind?"

I took a deep breath. I'd thought pretty hard about this. Realistically, I was getting paid six figures to do a job worth half that, while having sex with the hottest man alive. I would do the last for free, so really, I was way overpaid.

I couldn't very well tell Hunter that, though. He was a business prodigy the CEO of a huge, global company without even seeing thirty candles. He expected me to shoot high, and then barter hard.

I leaned forward and opened my mouth to spout out a ridiculous number when the phone rang. Hunter glanced at the display, then ripped the handset off the base. "Yes?"

I slowly closed my mouth and leaned back. The man could ignore a grenade blast if he had business to attend to.

"When is this?" Hunter asked with a sharp edge to his voice. He listened for a moment, checked his watch, and then clenched his jaw. "Who else will be there?" After another moment, he finished, "Get me booked in. Rearrange my schedule and move any meetings I can't miss to online. I need to be there."

He was about to put the phone back in the cradle when he paused. His eyes flicked to me. "Yes, she's going."

He set the phone down. "Negotiations will have to wait. The board has given me a limited time to secure a takeover. If I fail, which they hope I will, we'll go ahead with a merger. Donnelley—the owner and CEO of the prospective company…"

He waited for my nod before continuing, "He's attending a business summit at a resort in Nevada. This means he's shopping around for a buyer. He knows what his company is worth—or, more frankly, what its tech rights are worth—and he's ready to offload. He can't handle the size the company has grown to, so he's ready to cash out."

"Well…that's great, huh?" I asked, trying desperately to care. My brain was still lost on what he had planned for later that night.

"Yes, but he doesn't like me. He won't want to sell to

me if there's any way of avoiding it."

"Are there other companies willing to offer him as much as you?"

"A few." Hunter swiveled in his chair so he could gaze out the window. "My father's company, for one."

Intense loathing colored Hunter's voice. Saying he and his father didn't get along was putting it mildly. His dad was the root of Hunter's current distrust of others, distance from intimacy, and desire to be alone.

I was dying to know what had happened, but Hunter was an isolated, closed-off man. Getting at his depths would need the Jaws of Life.

I settled back in my chair. "If you don't get this takover, what's so bad about the merger?"

"A significant number of layoffs, organizational restructuring, which will drain our budget, and two leaders with vastly different long-term goals. I'll have to force my competition out, which will distract me from leading this company."

My eyebrows rose. "Then why does the board want a merger?"

Hunter shifted and looked back toward his computer. "Short-term gain, mostly. They estimate an increase in stocks, we'll have a larger market share, more reach—there are a great many reasons to do it, but an equal number of reasons not to. If we can get the takeover, on the other hand, we'll have more potential down the road. Most don't believe me, but I know I'm right. They're keeping me on a very short leash."

He faced me again and edged closer to his desk. "My father has a certain type of charm—he can manipulate people like no one else I've ever known. It's him I am competing against for this. He'll play the small business card—he'll say he built his company from scratch and knows the value of company loyalty. He'll talk about it like it's his child. He'll even say he wished his only son would've gone into business with him so he would have someone to pass his legacy on to. It's all crap, of course. But Donnelley will buy it, because my father will sell it. What I need is someone who *really* speaks Donnelley's language. Someone who is starting that uphill climb and trying to figure it out. Someone that loves her jeans and hoodies, just like Donnelley does…"

I raised my hand in the air and then dramatically pointed at myself. "I assume you mean *moi*?"

"Yes, you, Olivia," Hunter said. "You are my secret weapon. You're my charm. I need you to get me in. If he falls in love with you, and sees your loyalty to me, then hopefully he'll warm up to me."

"I don't know about falls in love with." I crinkled my nose.

Hunter's eyes sparkled. The edges of his lips tweaked, as close to a smile as he usually came. "We'll settle for deep respect, then." A stern expression crossed his face—his business mask. "We leave Wednesday, early. Plan for four days, maybe five. Pack some dresses—not too showy—and a large selection of casual clothes."

"Wednesday?" I gasped. I thought over the things I

would have to do before leaving. Like laundry, and coffee with Kimberly, and… My mind went blank.

Oh, that's right. I had no life.

"Okey-dokey, Wednesday it is." I bobbed my head.

"Use the rest of today to help Brenda get everything organized, learn what you can about Donnelley, and get prepared. You can take tomorrow off to get your personal things ready."

"Oh." I stood, glancing at the folder sitting open on his desk. "Okay."

"We'll talk money when we get back. If you land this, you'll have quite a bartering chip on your hands."

"I don't think bosses are supposed to tell subordinates how to get more money. It's not really in your budget's best interest…"

"I don't think subordinates are supposed to alert bosses when the bosses made a snafu regarding employee bartering…"

"Hmm. Right you are. Forget I said anything." I hopped up and turned to leave.

"And Olivia…"

I glanced back at Hunter expectantly.

"Check in before you leave."

Like a shock wave, a thrill arrested me. "Okay," I said in a breathy voice.

He turned back to his computer as I walked away stiffly. Once at my desk, I took a moment to gather myself. I couldn't wait to see what he was like when he could be completely in charge. When he didn't have to hold back for fear I'd pack up and leave.

With a shaking hand I reached for my mouse. Images of his naked body ran through my head, muscular and delicious. I closed my eyes as I remembered the feeling of him moving inside of me. It had been nearly three weeks. Much too long. I was going through withdrawals.

"Olivia—"

"Ah!" I jumped.

Brenda stared at me from her desk with her lips half turned up in a grin. "What's up with you?"

"You surprised me!" I clutched at my chest as my heart clattered against my ribs.

"I surprised you? I've been sitting here the whole time."

"Sorry." I looked harder at my computer. "I was thinking."

"What were you daydreaming about?"

"Your silence."

"Must've been juicy, whatever it was. Your face is giving you away…" Her grin turned evil. "It's a man, isn't it?"

I leaned toward my computer, staring hard at my email. There was no way I was admitting that I was slipping into dangerous waters with the boss. She'd just tell me all the reasons why it was a terrible idea. Like he was emotionally comatose and I'd get my heart ripped out. Or maybe that he had an arranged marriage set up, and even if he liked me, he was about to marry someone else. Just little things like that.

"Anyway, I'm working on the plans for that retreat," Brenda said. "Do you know what your role will be?"

"Wear jeans, act like a blue-collar worker, and get some business guy to like Hunter. Hunter apparently doesn't care that I'm mostly antisocial. Of all the people he chose to put his faith in…"

"I don't think he knows anyone else who wears jeans." She smirked. "It'll be fine. Mr. Carlisle hates to smile. He hates small talk. Compared to him, you're charming enough to be a politician."

"Is that supposed to be a compliment?"

Brenda's fingers flew across her keyboard. "Could be."

I scowled at her. That didn't sound promising.

"Anyway," she said, "I hope you can pull this guy out of the older Mr. Carlisle's back pocket—that guy gives me the creeps."

"Tell me about it. He all but asked me to be his mistress at that charity dinner."

Brenda's look was scathing. "Disgusting. He's old enough to be your father."

"And rich, which is all some women see. The girl with him was about my age."

"He wasn't with his wife?"

"He said they were getting a divorce."

Brenda tsked. "Typical. She probably grew too old for him. That's his third—no, wait." Brenda glanced at the ceiling, thinking. "The first was Mr. Carlisle's mother, then the maid, then…was there another one before this one?" She drummed the desk. "Yes, this must be his third. He was married to the maid for a while—just to put it in Mr. Carlisle's face, I'd wager. And he calls himself a father."

"To put it in Hunter's face?"

Brenda glanced at me. Wariness crossed her features. She glanced toward Hunter's opened door. Her voice lowered to a whisper. "I don't know much about it. Everything I heard comes from gossip, and *that* came from Mr. Carlisle senior, I think. Hunter has never said a word."

Brenda got up and moved closer, her coffee cup in hand. She glanced at the door to Hunter's office again. "Apparently—and again, this is hearsay—Hunter was in love with the maid. This was when he was young, maybe ten years ago. A little clichéd, I know." She rolled her eyes. "The word is that Hunter loved the maid, his dad found out, and then started having an affair with her himself. Well, she tried to leverage that connection somehow. It got ugly, from what I heard. Hunter's mother found out and threw a fit. She told all of their friends, all of Mr. Carlisle senior's work associates—you name it. I think Hunter was pretty sheltered as a kid—not many friends, not around many girls—so she was kind of it. And then she goes and betrays him… With his *dad,* of all people…"

She quirked her eyebrow and straightened up a little. Her lips pursed. "Damaging to a young guy. To his ego…"

"Yikes." I grimaced, but mostly for show. While that would definitely suck, and certainly be an ego crusher, it didn't smack me as reason enough for a life of cold business and solitude. It was a little weak on the "life trauma" Richter scale. There had to be more.

"You're telling me!" Brenda said, giving me a look before wandering back to her desk. "He's a good guy when you look past the rich-guy mentality. He just needs a hardheaded girl to break him out of his shell."

I snorted. "Good luck. He holds on to his rude *I know everything* act with both hands."

"That's a man for you." Brenda sat back down at her desk. "Do you need to go shopping at lunch, or are you going to take care of that tomorrow?"

"Shopping? Jeans and hoodies was my daily uniform before this job. I miss those days. Now I have to look around for a napkin when my hands are dirty."

"What does a napkin have to do with wearing jeans and a hoodie?"

"My jeans *were* my napkin. That's why they are so awesome—very versatile."

"Gross." I heard Brenda chuckling before the chorus of ticking announced her typing. "I'm ordering in lunch, then. Mr. Carlisle needs to give us a treat for working so hard."

"I'm all for free things."

"Aren't we all."

THE DAY PASSED in a blur of facts, figures, and strange

habits about a man I had never met. I felt like a private eye hired for a con. When Brenda shrugged into her jacket, I leaned back and rubbed my eyes. It was half past seven—late for her to be heading home.

"I thought you didn't do overtime?" I asked as she grabbed her purse.

"Usually, no. I don't want Mr. Carlisle to get accustomed to my being here all the time. But at crunch times, I put in the hours and take a half-day when the excitement wears off."

"Excitement, huh?" I smirked and glanced back at my computer. "I'll be working from home tomorrow, I think. I still have a bunch of things to get through."

Brenda paused on the other side of her desk. "Get ready for the trip first, and do work last. Mr. Carlisle has a bunch of meetings lined up when he gets to the summit that you won't need to attend. You can catch up then."

"So, lounge by the pool by day, and snuggle up to a perfect stranger at night. Sounds...weird."

Brenda barked out laughter. "Welcome to the job, girl. Welcome to the job."

She walked off to the elevators shaking her head. I scanned my spreadsheet one last time, retained nothing, and drooped against my desk. I was spent. As I didn't need a whole day to get ready tomorrow, I might as well call it a night and finish up later.

I pulled up my instant messenger and sent a note off to Hunter.

Olivia Jonston: I'm ready to head home…

A moment later, I received the reply:

Hunter Carlisle: Come in here. Lock the door behind you.

"Please," I muttered to finish his sentence. My stomach rolled and my sex tightened up. I glanced toward the elevators, making sure Brenda had gone. Then I smoothed out my clothes.

Oh God. This was it. I was about to waltz in, on command, and do whatever Hunter demanded.

I brushed my hair out of my face and then wiped my forehead of sudden perspiration. Tingles of nervousness worked through my body.

I was excited, yes. And horny as hell, but…I was going to give him the power. I was going to let him dominate me. It was terrifying. Exciting, but also terrifying.

Okay. Here goes.

I rolled my shoulders like a boxer. There was only one way to find out if I was comfortable with this.

I walked toward the office. Rabid butterflies ate away at my stomach. I stepped through the door.

Hunter sat at his desk, focused on his computer like he always was. Nothing in his demeanor had changed. His shoulders were relaxed. His movements were slow, almost lazy. He was completely at ease, utterly in his element. He was behaving as if the contract was in effect, I had no doubt.

I closed the door with a soft click, then turned the lock. Just him and me now.

Me at his mercy.

I walked toward him slowly, the flight reflex still tingling in my limbs. He looked up when I reached halfway and slowly leaned back in his chair. His gaze slid down my body before rising to meet my eyes. He pointed to his right at a space between his desk and the couch. "Stand over there."

Breathing became more difficult as the weight of expectation settled on my chest. Stiffly, more scared than thrilled, I made my way over.

I'd never submitted to anyone before. Not completely. I'd never given someone control like this.

What if I hate it? What will it mean for Hunter and me?

Hunter rose from his seat in a fluid movement. He shrugged out of his suit jacket, revealing his broad, muscular shoulders through the thin dress shirt. Once the jacket was laid across the top of his chair, he walked with slow, purposeful steps until he was right in front of me.

Topping my height by half a foot or more, he looked down into my eyes as his size overwhelmed me. His solidly built body oozed power and dominance. His eyes, hooded and smoldering, held his confidence and command, shocking into me and heating my core. His gaze roamed my face before settling on my lips.

"There's nothing to be nervous about, Olivia," he

said softly. "Any time you feel uncomfortable, just tell me to stop."

"Okay," I breathed, soaking in his heat and power. Sucking in the delicious scent of expensive aftershave and *man*.

He surveyed me for another moment, his eyes slipping down to my breasts before glancing at my throat. He bent slowly until his lips just glanced off the side of my neck. "Relax," he whispered.

His deep voice fizzled through my body as his lips softly touched my skin. Goosebumps spread from the point of contact until I shivered with desire.

"You'll like this." He lightly sucked a spot just over my pulse. "You'll like pleasing me."

My breath came faster. His presence, and his body, had me leaning forward, wanting his touch. Craving it. In the small space between us, electricity surged.

He straightened up again. His eyes delved deeply into me. "Take off my tie."

With shaking hands, I worked at the knot around his neck. I unraveled it and slid it from under his collar. I almost dropped it to the ground, but it was probably worth a couple hundred dollars, at least, knowing Hunter's tastes. I glanced around for the closest place to lay it down.

"Go put it on my jacket," he commanded.

I walked with a wobble, unsteady legs and high heels not being a great combination. I draped the silk on his tailored jacket and returned to the same place I had just left, determined not to take a step back and show my continued nervousness.

"Take off your clothes."

My whole body started to shake this time, adrenaline and anxiety creating something decidedly unsexy. If he noticed, though, he gave no sign as I undid the buttons down my front and stripped the material away from my suddenly perspiring body. I reached behind me for the zipper of my skirt, pushing the garment to the ground a moment later. I was too nervous to seek out somewhere to put my clothes—the ground was fine for them.

My face colored in embarrassment as I reached around behind my torso for my bra strap. I hesitated, unsure if I could do this. He was still fully clothed, watching me with passionate, heat-soaked eyes.

"Take it off, Olivia." His voice held the unyielding command that always managed to heat my skin and boil my bones.

Breath coming faster, I undid the clasp and closed my eyes as the material slid down my body and dropped to the floor.

"Good girl. Now your panties."

I can do this. I've undressed in front of boyfriends before. This is no big deal.

I hooked my fingers through the straps in my thong and pushed them down my hips. This was probably the unsexiest strip he'd ever seen in his life, but he didn't say anything. Didn't rush me. He just waited until I had let the lacy garment slip to my ankles and stepped out of them, teetering wildly as my balance swung off-center.

I felt a large, warm hand brace me until I was free of them, then it pulled away as I straightened up to stand on my own.

I was left in high heels. That was it.

My nipples constricted with both the cold air and increased anticipation. I looked up with a face that must have shown my embarrassment, and met his hungry eyes.

"Undo my shirt buttons, but don't take off my shirt."

I worked at the first, with trembling fingers, and took a deep breath. Focusing, I undid the top button, and worked on down, revealing a chest and stomach cut from a statue of perfection. His pecs were defined but not too big, leading down into abs so flawless they looked painted on.

Heat filled me. I wanted to bend forward and kiss those glorious abs.

"Undo my pants."

Metal jingled as I undid the clasp. The button was cold. I slid down the zipper, revealing blue boxer briefs straining with his bulge. I lightly traced the edges of the elastic band, his skin searing my fingertips. Unable to help myself, knowing I was stepping out of bounds, I let my fingers trace the grooves of his stomach. My body was revved up, hot and cold and needing to be touched.

"Take my cock out." His voice was tight. His breath ruffled my hair.

Hands steadier, body on fire, I reached beneath the

elastic and felt along his velvety skin. Gently, I pulled his hard shaft from its confinement, seeing his daunting size straining toward me.

"Get on your knees."

Another thrill coursed through me, but this time, it was all excitement.

I bent to my knees, more graceful than at any moment since I had locked the door. His prominent erection was at chin level. I salivated with the need to taste him. To slide my lips over his girth and hear him release a breath in pleasure.

"Look at me," he ordered.

I looked up and met those sexy, deep brown eyes filled with fire. "Suck my cock."

Without wasting any time, I grabbed his base as I licked around the tip. I lifted up and licked up the length before closing my eyes and taking him into my mouth.

"Look at me while you suck my cock, Olivia."

I let my gaze take the long way up, moving over his delicious upper body and shapely, full lips before meeting his eyes. Heat raged in me, squeezing my core and speeding up the plummet of my mouth on his erection. I took him in deep, past my gag reflex and into my throat. I'd only taken someone—him—that deeply once before, and hadn't mastered it. My throat tried to eject him and my eyes watered, but I pushed harder, watching his eyes flutter with the sensation of my mouth.

I backed off then, my hand trailing behind my mouth on his shaft, before taking him in again. And again. His body flexed, large muscles drawing my eyes. I sucked harder, moved faster, sliding my palm over his skin as my mouth took him in hungry gulps.

As his breathing became labored, his hand slid over my head and clutched my hair. He groaned right before he exploded in my mouth.

I slowed as he exhaled heavily. His muscles began to relax. I felt his hand drift down the side of my head and stroke my ear affectionately. A moment later, his body slumped.

When I was sure he was done, I let go, continuing to look up at him. Wanting him to tell me what was next, or if he had finished. Usually, with admins, he'd turn away. I expected that now.

He bent down and helped me up by my upper arms. He left his hands on me as he softly asked, "Do you want to clean up, or are you okay?"

"Are you finished?" I slid my hands up his torso, savoring the feeling of his smooth skin.

His eyes closed with a sigh. "Usually, yes, but…" His brow furrowed.

"I'll just visit the restroom. Why don't you sit on the couch?" I traced his lips with my fingers.

"I shouldn't," he whispered, a hint of fear starting to edge into his eyes. "I have work to do."

"You might get a second wind." I leaned forward and licked his nipple before sucking it in. His breath hitched.

"Okay," he said quietly.

I attempted a sexy saunter to the bathroom. Heels

had to be the devil's creation. If I wasn't hellbent on mastering the stupid things, I'd forget about them altogether.

Once in his private bathroom, I splashed water on my face, cleaned the smudges from under my eyes, and had a swig of his mouthwash. I figured using his toothbrush might be a bit brazen. Especially since I'd just…

When I walked back out he was sitting on the couch with his head resting against the back and his eyes closed. He'd removed all his clothes, including his socks, which was nice. Too often men forgot to take them off.

His eyes opened as I stopped in front of him. He looked up at me, pausing on my private areas before reaching my eyes. His manhood was at half-mast, already recovering.

"I thought you were a once-a-week kinda guy," I said, not really sure where to start. Hop on and go for a ride, or inch on slowly so as not to startle the prey? Decisions, decisions.

"Usually, I am."

I slid my legs over his slowly, relishing the feeling of skin on skin. I let my palms glide over his broad shoulders as my wet sex lined up with his stiffening manhood. He bent forward, kissing my neck before leaning me back to take a taut nipple into his mouth. He sucked in. Tendrils of pleasure wound down through my body. I closed my eyes as he switched nipples, moving my hips over his. His shaft, nearly hard again, worked between my nether lips, getting everything slick and ready.

"Hmm, Olivia," he said as he kissed up my chest and buried his face in my neck. "Fuck me."

A hard dose of desire pumped through me. I grabbed his hair and yanked his head back, staring down at his lips as I moved up, lining up his tip with my opening. I put my head down, seeing his fear as my lips neared his. His head jerked back a little and his eyes rounded. Whatever had happened with that maid, or someone else, Hunter Carlisle was terrified of being kissed on the mouth. Every time he thought that was coming, he shut down. A sick fascination kept me trying, though.

I veered toward his cheek as I sat down slowly, feeling him enter me. His size filled me up, pushing a long moan from my throat. My lips hit off his cheek before grazing his chin covered in coarse stubble. I lifted my hips and then sat back down, plunging onto him.

"Mmm," I sighed, gyrating upward as his hands squeezed my hips. I rose up and then sat down hard again, rocking the couch. I yanked his hair before biting his neck, needing a deep, passionate kiss and having to compensate in some other way for not getting it. I sat down harder, and again, increasing my pace. His manhood filled me, hitting places that made my eyes roll back in my head.

"Hunter," I breathed, rocking. "Ohhh."

His hands slid up my back and hooked on my shoulders, pulling me down harder. A jolt of pure pleasure shot through me. I clutched the back of the couch as he sat me down again, driving deep.

"Yes," I exalted, feeling the heat. Feeling the tightness. Winding up as waves of pleasure hit me. "Please."

My head fell back as I bounced on him, plunging him into me over and over. Our breathing filled the room. His hot mouth settled on my neck, and I gasped for breath as he pounded my body from beneath. The couch squeaked as we moved.

"Hunter…" I hugged his upper body as he leaned forward, encircling me in his strong arms. He stood with me clutching him, thrusting upward as I jerked my hips. The feeling of him, so big, so deep, had me begging, over and over, to climax.

He yanked my hair, ripping another moan from me, as he pumped into my body. I groaned and panted, the sparks of pleasure excruciating now.

"Please, Hunter," I said. Wanting us to come together. Wanting that command.

He thrust harder, two big pushes that had me unable to respond. I clutched tight, nails digging into his skin. Eyes squeezed shut.

"Come for me, baby," he commanded.

Everything exploded. My body flew apart, sizzling and burning, pleasure running through the cracks and covering me completely. I held on to him, shivering in ecstasy as he squeezed me to him.

My glorious climax drained away slowly, small bursts firing in succession before settling to a pleasant vibration in the aftermath. I melted around him, my arms dangling down his back as my head rested on his shoulder.

He backed up and sat on the couch, keeping himself inside me. He shifted me so my face was against his neck and my torso rested against his. A warm feeling rose up inside of me as I lay, feeling his heart beat against mine. His breath against my hair. His delicious smell on my skin. I sighed in contentment.

"I'll have to plan on taking more time with you—you've ruined my schedule for this evening," he said quietly.

"I wouldn't say ruined. A man with no life will probably hang around the office for a while longer."

"It sounded much more dramatic the way I said it." He kissed my temple. "I have to kick you out now, though."

"Okay." I lifted my face slowly and gave him a lingering kiss on the cheek. "But it was good while it lasted."

His brow was furrowed again as we got up and dressed. I could see him trying to shut down. Trying to turn off, as he was used to doing. Instead, he kept glancing at me, something working into his expression I couldn't read. Something like uncertainty. Or was it wariness? I needed the Hunter Carlisle cheat sheet to understand the man.

He finished dressing, giving me one last glance with that same furrowed brow before turning away. He walked to his computer without another word. Without a kiss or a hug or even a handshake. He was done, and I was dismissed.

I breathed through the uncomfortable hurt that I could not control. I knew this would come. This was his deal. He'd done it before.

Why did it suck so bad every time?

Taking a deep breath to clear that ache lodged in my middle, I finished dressing and turned to leave, trying to ignore the hollowness I felt.

"Olivia," Hunter said, his business voice, cold and calculating, dominating his tone.

I turned with raised eyebrows, waiting for him to continue.

He paused for a moment, with that same look working back into his eyes. "Stay online, if you would, or keep your phone close. I may need something before we leave."

"Yeah, sure," I said, forcing an easy-breezy tone.

As I left, I didn't hear any clicks of his mouse or ticks of the keyboard. I glanced back as I reached the door. His head was mid-turn. He'd been watching me walk from the room.

Chapter 2

O N WEDNESDAY, THE doorbell to my apartment rang as I was shoving clothes into my suitcase. I ran from my bedroom and slammed my index finger into the intercom button. "Hello?"

"Hey, Livy. It's Bert. You ready to go?"

"Damn it!" I said under my breath. Into the intercom I said, "Yeah. Be right there."

"I'll come up and help."

Of course he would. And then berate me for not being ready. Dang him for being so nice!

I pushed the button to open the outer door and left the apartment door open a crack before running back to my packing.

Yes, I should've been ready to go. And yes, I'd had yesterday off to do it. But I didn't want to let Hunter down. I wanted to land this business guy, and to do that, I had to know something about him. So yesterday, when I should've been getting ready, I was doing the equivalent of cramming for a test.

Well…that and daydreaming about Hunter. The man kept popping into my head whenever I had a second of idle time. Or when I was in the middle of something. Or…really, all the time. I couldn't get the guy out of my head. It was as pleasant as it was distracting.

I raced to my dresser and yanked open the top drawer. I grabbed undergarments willy-nilly. The silky nighties got balled with the cotton briefs and all got tossed into the suitcase.

"Livy?" Bert called from the entrance of my apartment.

"Yeah. Just…finishing up." I grabbed an old shirt to sleep in if I'd be alone and then silkier crap in case I was sleeping with Hunter. I really had no idea what to expect.

"Livy!" Bert stood in my doorway. "You're just packing *now*?"

"Just a few things I forgot." I snatched a few pairs of shoes and then stuffed them into the suitcase. I straightened up, my mind whirling. Undies, shirts, jeans, slacks, dresses…*socks!*

It had been a while since I wore runners—I needed socks. Fancy heels with jeans and a hoodie was not what I was going for.

"What were you doing yesterday?"

"I was working. I work too much, I know. Quit nagging!"

"I didn't say anything."

"You were thinking it."

Bert stepped forward as soon as the bag was zipped. "You're starting to sound like my wife."

"Well, now you know it's justified." I panted with fatigue.

Bert stepped out of the way so I could slide past him. "Crap!" I jogged into the bathroom and grabbed my toiletry bag.

"Makeup?" Bert asked.

"I got that. I have everything to look nice. I just forgot what I wear when I want to look dingy."

"Normal, Livy. When you want to look normal. I wish *I* could wear my jeans."

I smiled, leading Bert down to the street. "Hunter is leaving town. You'll get a couple days off."

"That'll be nice."

A traffic-clogged drive later, we met Hunter in front of his private jet. Large black letters spelling *Carlisle* were written on the side. He waited in fashionable jeans and a crisp white shirt that molded deliciously to his outstanding body. His hair was a messy sort of stylish, and a well-manicured five o'clock shadow adorned his handsome face.

I smirked when I walked up to him. "If you were trying to dress like a working man, you've failed miserably."

He looked down at his clothes. "Why? I'm wearing jeans, just like you."

"You are *owning* your extremely fashionable and ultra-clean jeans, not wearing them. You make those jeans actually *look* expensive, Hunter. That's talent."

A crease worked between his brows. He gestured toward the stairs leading up to the door of the jet. His stellar watch, which must have cost at least $15,000, sparkled in the light.

"The watch with the diamonds on the face was a nice touch, too." I laughed. "Nothing says *working man* like a fancy watch."

He didn't reply as he followed me up.

The trip to Nevada was short and quiet. Hunter had his head bowed over his computer, as did I. I did not want to blow this trip for him, and he didn't want to ruin this opportunity.

By the time we had finally reached our destination, a sprawling business complex about an hour outside of Las Vegas, we hadn't said more than a few words to each other. If I hadn't been so nervous about my role during this summit, that probably would've bothered me.

"Yes, Mr. Carlisle, thank you for joining us!" A man in his fifties smiled at Hunter from behind the check-in desk. Three large arrays of flowers shooting out of decorative vases dotted the countertop. Behind us in a greeting area, the size rivaling any Las Vegas hotel, sat a plethora of couches and chairs, and a couple of stations offering computer access. A TV spoke softly in the distant corner and a waft of soft music drifted from speakers in the ceiling.

"Okay..." The man laid out a piece of paper and immediately busied himself with plastic room keys.

"Two rooms, is that correct?"

"Yes." Hunter signed the forms and pushed them back across the counter before shifting his briefcase to his other hand. He stared at the man, his eyes hard.

That was his patient mask. No wonder people thought he was angry all the time.

"All righty, here we go." The man laid two sets of keys on the counter in their little sleeves, open to the room number. "Second floor, rooms three-oh-five and three-fifteen."

Hunter pushed the keys back toward the man. "No. The rooms need to be next to each other, adjoining if possible."

"I am so sorry, sir—I see that in the notes here. Just a moment." The man took to his computer with a knot in his brow. In just a moment, he nodded and clicked the mouse. "No problem. We'll have to move you to rooms at the rear of the compound, but that can be arranged easily."

"The rear of the compound?" Hunter asked.

The man looked up with a smile. "Yes, sir. Just to the back. You are a little further away from the heart of the hotel, but the rooms are bigger. Golf carts are at your disposal if you want to see the grounds."

"Oooh, yay!" I blurted.

Hunter looked at me, confusion clouding his gaze. A moment later, his face cleared and the hint of a smile worked at his lips. He turned back to the desk. "Fine."

I let my attention wander as someone came through

the front door. I recognized the tall, handsome older man immediately, walking in like he owned the hotel and the world it was built on. Rodge Carlisle, Hunter's father.

"Have a good stay!" The man at the counter beamed.

"Hunter," I said quietly.

He looked at me before following my gaze. His body stiffened and his eyes took on a hard edge. He turned back to me. "Let's go."

Rodge saw me then, and gave that charming smile that opened doors and fooled the unbelievers. His eyes twinkled. He winked at me.

I gave him a scowl before turning away. I didn't really have a reason to hate him—making a pass at me didn't make most people a mortal enemy—but my allegiance was to Hunter, and if Hunter hated the man, then I was on board. Brenda didn't like him either. Done and done. My you-suck face was in full effect!

I followed Hunter through the large foyer and into a hallway, trusting he knew where we were going. We left the building through a glass door and slowed as we reached the heart of a large garden, turning a harried pace into a stroll. The smell of flowers and foliage greeted me. The weak late-fall sun sprinkled down, but it was not enough to erase the desert chill.

"No pool for me—too cold." I shivered and crossed my arms. I should've brought a thicker sweater.

Hunter glanced over as we ambled along a winding path. "Wrong time of year."

"Yes, it would seem," I said in a dry voice.

"Hot tub."

"Then your father would probably hop in wearing purple Speedos or something. No thanks."

I meant it as a joke, but Hunter's shoulders tightened at the mere mention of his dad. He slowed to a stop, eyes rooted to a cactus. "Olivia, I think you should know that I'm not exactly rational where it comes to my father. Some scars run too deeply. So if…" His jaw clenched. He slipped one of his hands into his pants pocket. "If you flirt with him, or spend time with him, I'm not sure I'll react…professionally."

I laid my hand on Hunter's arm. His head tilted toward me fractionally, but he didn't turn to meet my gaze. "The man is old, he's a total fake, and he gives me the heebie-jeebies. Trust me, I'm not going to swan-dive into a conversation with him if I can help it, let alone *flirt.*"

Hunter shifted a little. His arm brushed against mine as he continued to look at the prickly plant. Without thinking, I slipped my hand around his arm and leaned against him.

"What'd he do?" I asked softly.

I felt Hunter stiffen again before he pulled away and returned to a hurried pace.

"So, that question is off-limits, I take it," I mumbled as I followed after him.

We reached a large square area where two neat lines of golf carts stood.

He walked toward the one on the end. "You can

drive us. I want to think over the best way to make contact with Donnelley."

Like a kid getting handed a piece of candy, I crawled into the cart with a huge smile. I stowed my laptop behind me and checked out the controls. There was a key, a gas pedal, a brake pedal, and a couple buttons—probably lights and a horn. I turned the key, placing my hand on the shifter next to the wheel when it shimmied to a start.

He climbed in and rested his briefcase on his lap.

"Ready?" I asked, pushing the gear to "D."

"Take it away, Dale Earnhardt, Jr."

Laughing, I stepped on the gas and we lurched to a start. "Touchy, this thing."

"When was the last time you drove?" he asked, grabbing the handle on the dash.

"Um…five years ago, I think. I didn't have a car in college."

"Have you ever owned a car?" He pointed to the right. I couldn't read what the sign posted on the corner of the grass said, but turned that way, anyway. Obviously he knew where he was going. And if not, it didn't matter. It was only a golf cart, but it was fun.

"I sold it for some college money."

"Excuse me if this is too personal, but your mother didn't help you?"

"She didn't help, no. She's…a bit self-centered. She grew up with a mother exactly the same, with the same affinity for married men. Some people become the opposite of how they were raised, and some…don't.

"She had two brothers—who I've never met. Being the youngest, with a mostly absent mother, she had to fend for herself a lot. They were cash poor and property rich, so when her mother died, she inherited a lot of property. Most she sold, then blew. So now she hoards what little she has left. She dates rich men and she keeps up with plastic surgery—paid for by the rich men."

"And you don't blame her." Hunter wasn't asking a question, he was making a statement.

I shrugged. "I do, in some ways. But she's a product of her childhood. I've stopped trying to understand my mother, and blaming her won't change who I am now."

"And you?"

I followed his pointed finger to the path on the left. "I'm my father's daughter. And he was a very loving, giving man. I was an accident. My mom didn't want my dad—he wasn't rich or anything. Handsome, but that's about it. She was having fun, and the fun caught up with her."

"And he passed a few years ago, correct?"

"Right after I got accepted to Stanford, yes. I've never seen him more proud." Tears blurred my vision, as I remembered his beaming smile even though he was pretty sick with cancer at that point. "He always told me that I was his life's treasure. That he hadn't known what love was until I was put into his arms. I miss him."

Hunter was silent for a while. Finally he said, "And what happened after he passed?"

"I was mostly on my own."

"That must've been hard. Especially without funds."

I shrugged again, pulling up in front of a sprawling building with a few golf carts parked haphazardly out front. I parked beside the closest and shut off the engine. "I had a few grants that I used for living expenses and worked a few hours in the library, so I made do. At the time I thought the overpriced education would open doors to fabulous and high-paying jobs…"

"Bad timing. A few years earlier, and it would have."

"Yeah, that's what Kimberly says every time she buys me lunch." I climbed from the seat and grabbed my computer. "Although I did land a high-paying job, regardless of the field, so I have that going for me."

"Except for the additional requirements asked of you in the name of some rich man's whim…"

I glanced at Hunter as he opened the door for me. His expression was completely blank. It didn't match the heavy tone he'd just used.

"I wouldn't do it if I didn't want to, Hunter," I said as we entered the building.

We walked through the plush halls in silence. Decorative sconces lined the walls and a busy pattern confused my eyes underfoot.

We twisted and turned through the corridors until we reached rooms 1022 and 1023. Hunter opened 1023 and once again held the door, following me in after. The room opened up before me in an abundance of hotel elegance. A king-sized bed sat against the far wall, a huge desk squatted in the corner, a chair in the other corner, a couch near the door—the one room was the size of my bedroom in San Francisco and adjoining living room, both. Maybe even the eating area. It was huge!

"Jeez—why would you think I needed this much space?" I wandered in, walking to the right to look in the empty closet before peeking in the adjacent bathroom.

"Your bags should be here any moment."

I emerged as Hunter was undoing the catch on an interior door on the side. Once opened, another white door barred the way—the one to his room. He faced me from beside the door. "Whenever you want privacy, go ahead and close this."

"Yes, because it's a door. It closes…"

He ignored my sarcasm, staring at me with an unreadable expression. "Olivia, I have to ask. How do you feel about Monday?"

Goosebumps spread across my body as I realized what he was talking about. My cheeks heated. "It felt good. I wanted it."

His eyes delved into mine. "I realize you aren't like the others. You didn't accept these conditions for monetary or even professional gain. You're in a dangerous place, Olivia. I'm not a man who feels. My intimacy is a distant thing, at best. I don't love, and you have no future with me. I'm not good for you."

I folded my arms over my chest as uncertainty washed over me. "What are you saying?"

A glimmer of helplessness entered his gaze. "I can't

give you what you're going to want. But I won't push you away, either. I'm selfish and I want you, but I'll just keep taking and taking until I use you up. I need you to understand that. I need you to understand the danger you're in."

"So…" I shifted to my right side, confusion and rejection dragging down the corners of my mouth. Heat prickled the back of my eyes, tears at the ready. It felt like a breakup. "Are you firing me, or what?"

"No. This conversation is to absolve me of guilt. I'm sexually attracted to you in a way I haven't been with anyone in a very long time. Possibly ever. I'd take you every day if I could. And I might. But I'm a soulless, heartless bastard who shuts off once he's taken what he wants. That's just the way it is. I won't lie with you and cuddle all night. I won't be able to love you, Livy. So if that's not something you can handle, I'll respect it if you take a job elsewhere in my company. I'll set you up with whatever you need."

Unshed tears coated my eyes. It felt like he was ripping something from inside me that I barely realized he'd planted in the first place. I let my hands fall to my side. Now I knew, for sure, that he would steamroll me by the time this was all through.

The question was, was the journey to love, no matter how it ended, more important than keeping the object of my affection? Because I was absolutely on that road. He knew it too, and I'd gotten a taste of it yesterday when all I could think about was seeing him again. I had to experience more of him, because in my heart, I knew he had so much more to offer.

Except he's not willing to offer it to you, Olivia!

I looked away as a tear made its way down my face. I sighed in helplessness. "You won't push me away, and I won't walk away on my own, so I guess we'll just have to see where it ends."

"We know where it will end," he said softly.

"Then so be it."

Hunter stared at me for a moment. He opened his mouth to speak, but stopped at a knock on the door. He moved, and admitted the bellboy with a cart of luggage. Hunter arranged for the right bags to be brought in before tipping the man.

He held the door open as the man wheeled Hunter's own bags to the room next door. Hunter glanced at the inside door before letting his gaze settle on me again. "Use that door when you need some privacy. I'll leave mine open in case you need something. I have to be in a conference in an hour, so I would advise you to take your computer and stroll through the grounds. Meet people. Make friends. You never know who you might need to accomplish your goals."

Another tear fell. I looked down at my bags as I rubbed my face before running my fingers through my hair. It wasn't a good cover, but it was all I had.

"Try to shut yourself off from me, Olivia," Hunter advised softly. "Try to distance yourself, and think of this for what it is—experience and great sex."

"I don't work like that. I can't separate my heart from my life. It stops me from being a whole person."

"I know," he whispered. And he stepped away. The door closed with a dull *thunk*.

I heaved a breath and blinked, trying to rid myself of tears. I rubbed at my chest where my heart was seeping, aching painfully.

I looked at my luggage for a long time, remembering the various looks I'd gotten from Hunter over the time I'd known him. I knew he was scared of love, and afraid of intimacy, because of whatever lurked in his past, but the deep passion he expressed in tender moments, and the openness he'd displayed, meant he was capable of it. I had to believe that.

Maybe just not with me.

I shook my head as a metal latch hit against wood. The connecting door swung open, revealing a muscular shoulder in a button-down shirt moving away on the other end. He'd said his piece, given me the warning I'd heard a few times before, and that was that. He was clear.

I wished it were that easy for me.

I took a quick shower to waste some time before climbing into my battle gear—jeans and a hoodie. Hunter said I could wear what I liked, so I chose a loose-fitting gray hoodie to complement my dour mood. I peeked into Hunter's room, only to find it empty.

I dusted myself with makeup and threw my hair in a ponytail. I didn't need to try very hard to get that look. I probably wouldn't see Donnelley, since the grounds were so big, and definitely wouldn't randomly make friends. Like a stereotypical geek, I was more comfortable in a corner somewhere with my computer, avoiding contact with anyone else.

I grabbed the plastic key off the little stand by the door and shoved it in my pocket before heading out with my computer. I found my golf cart right where I left it. Hunter must've walked. I climbed in and started her up with no idea of where I was headed. I just followed paths willy-nilly, until I found a lovely little spot with non-native trees, non-native flowers, and definitely a non-native little lagoon surrounded by benches and tables. Maintaining the integrity of the Nevada desert was not important with this little setup.

I shut off the engine and climbed out, lugging my ever-faithful computer with me. Two people sat at tables on opposite ends of the lagoon. I headed for one of the tables between them. As I passed the nearest man, though, I caught sight of his face.

I did a double take. My foot caught a rock and had me stumbling to the side with a loud grunt.

Donnelley looked up.

Of *course* I'd find Donnelley. I had to, right? With my luck, there was no way that I would get to sit on my own and reflect on Hunter's words. That would have been too easy.

I pointed vaguely at the ground. "Rocky."

His focus dipped down to his hands where he held a phone. A man in his late fifties, he had graying hair and life's wear and tear lining his face. Frustration painted his visage. His laptop was pushed away to one side.

Now to make contact.

"You…ah… Everything okay?" I'd never been good at initiating friendship.

Chapter 3

H E GLANCED UP in irritation. Great, I was already annoying him.

"No. Just—" He shook his phone a little. "This blasted thing isn't picking up a signal." His eyes were crisp and blue, sparkling with intelligence and anger. "I design programs that sell like hotcakes on these things, but I can't even work it."

"Oh. Um…" I shuffled closer. I should try to help. That was a good *in.* I just wished I wasn't so awkward about it.

It felt like high school all over again as I leaned over the table trying to get a peek at what he was doing. I expected him to pull the phone away from my prying eyes any moment and tell me to buzz off.

I vaguely pointed again. "Looks like you're in that weird place between Wi-Fi and phone signal…"

Donnelley glanced up with a furrowed brow. He looked back at his phone. I was annoying him.

Hunter would pay for this.

I tried again. "The phone is barely picking up Wi-Fi from the hotel. So then it tries to switch to the phone signal, but…it looks like that's weak here too. When it's in that weird place when neither signal is strong enough, it's useless."

He nodded impatiently as irritation crossed his face again. Thankfully, this time it didn't seem to be because of me. "I didn't even notice. Lamebrain."

I tried to hide my smile at the term originating decades before. I looked at my phone face. I had all kinds of service. "I thought this hotel had a booster for service."

"It does for Verizon. I have AT&T."

"Oh. Well, I'm all set then." I gave him a feeble laugh, wanting to wander away. I'd not really helped, I'd overstayed my welcome, and I was terrible at small talk. But I had to hang around. This was awful.

I offered my phone with a smile that I hoped hid my gawkiness. "You can use my phone. My boss pays for service, so download whatever you want."

His hand jerked in what looked like reflex. He paused with it nearly to my phone and looked up. "Are you sure? I just need to check a couple things. We've had a couple complaints with the app and I was just trying to work them out."

"No, no—have at it." I pushed it at him eagerly. "I'll just be over there." I jerked my head to the picnic table I had picked out.

"Please, sit here." He motioned toward the seat opposite him as he grabbed the phone. "That way you can tackle me if I wander off with it."

I glanced back at my chosen spot, blessedly free of small talk and polite interaction, but when I looked back he was already bent over my phone. My presence might've completely disappeared for all he seemed to notice me.

Without further hesitation, I sat. "You have the same single-minded focus as my boss."

His thumbs flew over the screen. No comment.

With a small huff and a smile, I opened my computer, starting to relax. "You ignore me just like Hunter, too. Fabulous," I muttered sarcastically, clicking in the wireless USB.

"Hunter…Carlisle?" Donnelley glanced up.

I let my smile grow, now in acting mode. I didn't look up from my computer. He'd probably appreciate that. "Mr. Carlisle, yes. When he's concentrating really hard, he might as well be deaf."

"You called him Hunter?"

As my email pulled up, I looked up at him. "Hunter, yeah."

"Hmm." Donnelley pulled his computer closer. "I hadn't realized anyone used Mr. Carlisle's first name. The son, I mean."

"Maybe it's because I'm born and raised Californian and we're more laid-back."

Donnelley cracked a smile before straightening his back and stretching. "Got it. Maybe we won't have as many one-star reviews on that game."

"Which game is it?"

Donnelley passed my phone back. I saw the picture of a cartoon rat. "Oh my God—this is *your* game?" I knew that already, of course. I'd be a terrible researcher if I didn't.

His eyes twinkled in delight. "Yes. I saw you already had it on your phone. And you play it."

It was a puzzle game where the player was supposed to alter the route of the maze to get the mouse through. I'd actually found it randomly before Donnelley's name ever came up, and had been playing it off and on since. "I play when I need to let my mind go dead."

Donnelley clasped his hands on the table. "What did you say you did?"

"I'm an admin right now, but I majored in computer engineering. I'm Olivia. Or Livy, if you want."

"Bruce." He extended a large, grizzled hand with a collection of scars and old calluses. His handshake was firm, but not hard. He was probably easing up because I was a woman. And for that, I was thankful.

"Those aren't a computer man's hands, Bruce," I said as I took my hand back.

"I spent my youth pushing a shovel. Had to pay the bills while I was playing with my computer."

"Ah." I held up my hands. "Computer girl's hands. I can't write worth a damn, but I type like the wind."

He laughed. "I'm an experienced hunt and pecker, to this day. I tried the traditional approach, but it felt like selling out."

I glanced at my computer as an email came in. It was Hunter, scheduling me for a meeting in two weeks. I sighed, opening the email and reading about an entirely new subject. Which meant, after this weekend, I'd have a whole new set of urgent requests from my fearless leader to deal with.

"What is it?" Bruce asked. "If you don't mind me asking."

"Oh." I pointed at my screen in a show-and-tell moment, even though he couldn't see it. "While I am here, I'm trying to help keep Hunter's schedule in line, and he's sitting in a lecture somewhere, planning completely unrelated meetings weeks in advance about topics he's never discussed with me. It keeps me on my toes."

"And…pardon me again for intruding, because I am a nosy bastard, but you don't seem overly put out. You like working for him?"

I scanned the email and shook my head. I'd have to start looking at budgets. What a pain.

"No?"

I started, remembering what I was supposed to be doing. Bruce was staring at me with a calculating gaze.

"Sorry." I got my mind back on track. "Yes, I do. It was tough at first because he's so focused, but once you get to know him, he's a great boss." I told Bruce about the company perks that Hunter constantly fought the board for, and our ability to buy clothes on his dime. I also told him about the car service and buying lunch whenever we felt we needed it. When I was done, I returned to my computer in a nonchalant sort of way. I was a terrible salesperson. The best thing I could do was state the facts and feign indifference, otherwise Bruce would know I was trying to push Hunter's awesomeness.

"He buys your clothes…" Bruce glanced at my faded hoodie.

"Not this." I pinched my sweatshirt with a sheepish smile. "I got to dress like normal today. I wasn't supposed to see anyone I knew. Or…you know…that knew who I was. He buys the stuff I wear to the office. Or like tonight, dresses to events. His driver gets a suit. Things like that."

"Ah." Bruce was still looking at me with that calculating gaze.

I stared back. "Don't judge. It's like playing dress-up. Girls like this sort of thing."

A grin worked at his lips. He threw up his hands in surrender. "I'm not judging. It's like a uniform."

"Exactly." I gave a decisive nod. "A uniform that the boss has to pick out because I have absolutely no fashion sense."

"Oh, I don't know, that sweatshirt is a pretty popular style…"

I glanced down at my chest, trying to look busy and important. "I know what the poor kids are wearing, yes. I've got that down pat."

Bruce leaned back and looked around him. "Hunter represents one of three companies that are trying to buy me out."

"Oh? And why are you selling?"

"Another Nosy Parker." Bruce's smile didn't reach his eyes. "It's gotten too big for me. I work all the time. My wife is pissed, I don't see my kids anymore—it's no life."

"I wouldn't know. I work a lot precisely *because* I have no life."

This time, his eyes sparkled with humor. "You will one day. And when you do, you'll realize the important things in life aren't money and the office."

"Can you, maybe, take a step back in your duties? That way you could still hang on to it…"

I grimaced. I'd said it before I could run it through my filter. It was the opposite of what I was going for.

"I tried. That's what I was supposed to be doing this year. But I was distracted all the time, wanting to be in the office when I wasn't, having to clean up messes—it wasn't working. I'm too old for it now. Time to pass the torch."

I nodded in understanding, looking at the table. "Sucks."

"Tell me about it."

"So you have three business guys breathing down your neck."

Bruce closed his computer with a click. I thought I'd just ended the conversation, but instead, he leaned his elbows on the table and looked over at the lagoon. "Exactly. One mammoth company, and two large companies. Hunter has the deepest pockets, but he's…the job. He's a bright kid, I'll give him that, but he doesn't have the years of experience the others do."

"Even those with experience have to answer to their company's board members. Really, the winner is who can push their ideas past the stockholders."

"True. I couldn't even imagine that kind of hassle."

"I couldn't before this job. Now I'm getting a glimpse. Hunter has all these plans years out. *Years!* Don't ever play chess with the man, seriously." I threw up my hands. "I can't think that far ahead. I just can't. I'm more of an 'in the moment' type of girl. Maybe a month out, but that's it. Planning isn't my specialty. Maybe someday, but…"

"And yet you are trying to keep track of his scheduling…"

"Yeah!" I barked out laughter. "I'm no good at it, though. Joke's on him, right? It's like trying to direct a river barge up a stream. I want to pull my hair out half the time, and punch him in the mouth the other half."

Bruce gave a large belly laugh. His deep, delighted rumble had the man across the lagoon looking over. "Why are you in the job, then?"

"I just got the job—a month ago. I graduated six months back. You do that math."

"Oh. A product of the economy, huh?"

"Exactly. All the clubs and extracurricular actives look good on the résumé, but not half as good as some experience. Call me enlightened. It's okay, though. His other assistant, Brenda, does most of the heavy lifting with the admin stuff. I get random jobs."

"So Hunter gave you a chance and is now playing to your strengths…"

I glanced at my screen as another email came in. "Stop sending me stuff," I muttered, minimizing the window. I turned back to a smiling Bruce. "I think he's happy to have someone that can do more than admin. And I'm happy to get paid, so we can use each other for a while."

"No harm in that. And you seem to be learning…"

"It's good, but there's always a moment of frustration when he gives me something new."

Bruce got up and slipped his phone in his pocket. "Well, I have to run. Thanks for letting me use your phone. Download the update—let me know what you think."

"Gaming isn't your business, though, right?" I asked, pulling my phone closer.

"No. Another hobby. One that makes money."

"Must be nice, being smart."

"You should know." Smiling, he sauntered away.

I gave myself a mental pat on the back. I had given him something to think about, even though I had been a little heavy-handed. At least now I could work on him. Or just introduce Hunter and do a little damage control.

My mind went back to my comment about using each other. That statement might've been a little one-sided.

Glad to be on my own again, I got lost in my work.

What I'd said was true—Brenda did most of the admin stuff. So I pulled up the marketing spreadsheet I'd been working on, and got lost in analysis.

I finally came out of my spreadsheet fog as a chill breeze prickled my skin. I took a deep breath and looked around. The guy that had been on the other side of the lagoon was gone and I was alone.

I glanced at the clock. "Oh crap!"

It had been three hours! I was supposed to be ready for dinner in an hour and a half. That seemed like plenty of time, but I always seemed to mess up at least one part of my wardrobe.

I packed everything up and jammed my computer into its bag. I hurried to the golf cart and put it into gear, lurching to a start. It took me thirty seconds to come to a horrible realization—I didn't know how to get back!

I'd taken turns without a thought to the way back.

Well, now I was in a pickle.

I squinted at the upcoming sign. "Rec room →"

"Rec room?" I muttered. Out here in the middle of cultivated gardens and nondescript buildings, and they thought the *rec room* was the most important directional tool?

I thought about calling Hunter as I zoomed along the path and around a couple people on foot, one in a suit, the other in jeans.

"Livy?"

I slowed and craned in my seat, recognizing the voice. Sure enough, Bruce looked at me quizzically with a twisted grin on his face. He and a businessman with a frustrated expression stopped next to me.

"Practicing for the Indy 500?" Bruce asked with twinkling eyes.

"I'm totally lost!" I said. Then couldn't help a laugh. "But yes. This thing's a hoot!"

"We'll have to race one of these times. Where ya headed?"

"I'm in room 1023. Any ideas?"

"You're just…" The businessman squinted off to the left. He stuck out his hand and pointed. "Just there, I think. That way."

He assumed I could fly, apparently, because he was pointing straight at a gazebo and a bunch of bushes.

"Here's a map. Can you read maps?" Bruce held out a crisp, folded paper.

"Have you even used this?" I asked, taking it. I opened it up and then turned it around, trying to get my bearings.

"No, but I'm good with direction." Bruce moved up next to me. "Here you are." He pointed at a picture of a fountain.

"But where's the—" I cut off as I noticed the land-mark some distance in front of us. There was no water running through it to announce its presence. "Ah. Got it."

"Okay. Then you just…" Bruce pointed out the route with his finger. "Just follow that route."

I took a glance around to make sure I had it, and

then gave him a relieved smile. "Lifesaver! I'm supposed to be getting ready for dinner."

"Back into uniform, huh?" Bruce stepped away with a smile. The businessman was still glowering at me.

"Yup. Gotta play dress-up. Okay, then. See ya. And thanks!" I gave him a salute and stomped on the gas. I probably shouldn't have kept speeding but…well, it was fun.

At least I had met Bruce. That was a win. Assuming he didn't think I was a lunatic.

Chapter 4

A KNOCK SOUNDED at the outer door to my room.
Crap! I finished fastening my necklace and hurried to open it, glancing at the closed inner door as I passed. The comment about Hunter and I using each other had popped into my head. Knowing that it was mostly him doing the using, I'd huffed and closed that inner door. It was an extremely passive-aggressive approach to the issue, but it had made me feel better.

I swung open the outer door to a waiting Hunter in stylish jeans and a dress shirt accenting his delicious torso. He'd styled his hair in that contained messiness that celebrities did so well, and cleared the stubble from his strong jaw. My tongue stuck to the roof of my mouth as the blackness of my mood turned into sparkles and unicorns.

"Hi," I breathed.

"Are you ready?" His gaze drifted down my body.

I stalled in the doorway. I wanted to invite him in and strip off all his clothes. Then I wanted to lick one end to the other, savoring—

"Olivia?"

"Right! Earrings." I shook myself out of my horny stupor and dashed back into the room. I grabbed the diamond earrings he'd given me. He had the necklace in a safe somewhere, which was good, because it was way too expensive to be hanging around my apartment, but the earrings he'd left. He didn't seem to think they had much value.

They were the most expensive things I owned.

"Okay," I said, fastening the last earring in place. "I'm as good as I'll ever be."

"Shoes?"

"What?" I looked down. My bare toes stared back up. *Stupid!*

I raced back in a second time. Where was my head?

I slipped into cute red heels that would cut into my feet and make me hate life. But they really did match the dress perfectly. Some things had to be borne.

"Okay. This time I'm really ready."

"You're perfect." He stopped me in the doorway, stepping in a bit and leaning down to run his lips along my neck. My simmering sex flared to life. I clutched his shoulders and leaned my head back, giving him more access. The *using each other* grievance vanished like smoke.

His hand traced up my inner thigh, tickling. I widened my stance, moaning when those tricky digits reached my panty-covered sex.

"Hmmm, Hunter." His lips traced my jaw. His fingers dipped into my panty line. I sucked in a breath as he entered my body.

"The door is open," I said in a breathy exhale.

"I need you." He stepped forward, making me step back quickly. The door closed with a *thunk* as he pushed me against the wall.

I worked at his jeans, ripping open the fly and pushing them out of the way. His hand wrapped around the inside of my knee and hiked my leg up around his hip. He sucked in a breath as I took his large manhood into my hand. His hips swung forward, letting me guide his tip to my opening. Once there, he thrust.

"Ohhhh *God.*" My eyes fluttered closed as he filled me. I lifted my other leg, wrapping it around him. Letting him take my weight. Sparks of pleasure erupted through my body.

"I've thought about doing this all afternoon." He thrust again. Harder. "It always feels better than I remember."

I turned my head as he came in close. My lips glanced off his. A thrill went through me as Hunter gave a low moan. My body wound up, so tight. His sex, filling me over and over, had bursts of ecstasy exploding through me.

"Yes," I groaned, swinging my hips to him. Our bodies hit off each other. Everything tightened harder. Almost unbearable.

"Oh *G*—" I squeezed my eyes closed as pure bliss

sizzled through me. I vibrated with the climax. Hunter shook under me, moaning again. Pings of delight burst and then ran my length, fizzing.

"Holy moly." I sighed as I came down. "That felt good."

Hunter lowered me to the ground. He straightened my panties and dress before tucking himself back into his pants. His chest rose and fell with fatigue. Before he turned away, he looked at me for a long moment. His hand braced against my jaw. He kissed my forehead.

He gave me one last glance, then looked at himself, before opening the door. "Ready?"

I was speechless. He hadn't shut off. Even right now, as he waited for me to exit the room, his eyes were soft and fully engaged. He wasn't struggling to let business cover physical intimacy.

"Olivia?"

"Sorry! Yup." I jumped to a start and hustled out of the room in case he fell back into his own ways with my delay.

"That's twice you were zoning out tonight. What's on your mind?"

You! "Nothing. Just trying to remember everything I need to do while we're here."

"Don't stress. Brenda is on call. She's monitoring everything. You just need to work on Donnelley."

"Well, then, I'm throwing aces. I saw him twice to-day."

Hunter opened the building door and put his hand

on the small of my back to guide me through. "He said. Apparently you tested the limit of the golf cart…"

"Oh. Uh…" My face went hot. "I got lost. And was hurrying. So…"

Hunter escorted me to the golf cart and deposited me on the passenger side.

A little disappointed, I climbed in.

"Men drive on dates."

My stomach fluttered. "I thought this was business."

He started the golf cart and smoothly started forward. "A business date, then. An excuse to take out a beautiful woman. Whatever you want to call it."

"Very unprofessional." I laughed.

"Did you get everything done this afternoon?" Hunter asked after a moment of silence. He parked near the line of golf carts beside the main building.

"Yup. And don't you dare ask if I looked at those new emails you sent—I did, and they make no sense. I'll deal with them when I get back."

"Fair enough," he said, holding the hotel door open.

"So you talked to Bruce, then?" I said as I entered. "You didn't need me after all."

I felt Hunter's guiding touch on the small of my back. Without thinking, I veered closer to him, feeling his heat line my side and soak through my skin. His hand slid, just a little, to the side, nearing my waist to pull me closer. Warmth turned to fire.

"He approached me. Said you were a smart young woman." Hunter directed us around a corner. The hallway widened until it ended at the entrance of a steakhouse.

"Oh, did you see him in one of your lectures?"

"Briefly. He took a seat closer to my father. You loosened him up, but he thinks my father will protect his hard work. He's fallen victim to my father's charms."

"What charms? I just don't see it."

"You haven't been around him long enough."

"I've been around him plenty," I said in a dry voice as we approached the hostess waiting behind a lectern.

"Carlisle. Hunter." Hunter stared at the woman.

"Oh, yes, of course." Her face colored. She smiled bashfully at his smoldering stare. "Please, right this way."

"Do you hate it when women see you as a piece of meat, or do you love being a sexpot?" I shot him a grin over my shoulder. He ignored my jest.

Dim light and the smell of searing steaks greeted us. I had no doubt the food would be decent and prices absurd, like many chain restaurants in places like this. Still, it was better than fast food.

We sat in the corner at a table for four. The hostess, shooting furtive glances at Hunter and ignoring me completely, dropped the menus on the table. "Your server will be right with you."

Hunter held my chair out before sitting opposite me. He glanced around the restaurant before letting his gaze settle on me. "You don't look as casual as I thought you might…"

"I'm at dinner." I gave him a faux-scathing look. "I

can't look like a street urchin at dinner. I'm not *that* bad."

"What were you wearing today?"

"Hoodie. Jeans. Hair in a ponytail. You know, my street uniform."

He gave me a single nod before glancing at his menu. I followed suit, though I knew I'd be getting filet mignon. No way was I passing up the opportunity for an excellent cut of meat—why not go big when the boss was paying? Finding what I wanted, I set the menu aside.

"Do you own anything but dress shirts?" I asked, glancing out at the restaurant. Patrons filled most of the space, many also wearing dress shirts, a few in ties, and only a couple completely dressed down in T-shirts and jeans. Those few stuck out a little—possibly not here for the convention and wondering why the place was inundated with businessman.

Hunter looked down at his chest. A crease worked between his eyebrows. "I rarely have need for anything but dress shirts."

"And now that you do, what are you? Too dressed up, that's what."

Hunter glanced at my red dress and sparkling jewelry. His mouth tweaked, hinting at a smile. "I match my company."

Not even remotely. I saw the waitress approaching. Still, she only had eyes for Hunter. And once again, he didn't even notice that she practically had to wipe drool off her chin while he was ordering. The whole situation was becoming comical.

"Just wait. If we ever get a male waiter, I'm going to dazzle him to the point of distraction. I might even bat my eyelashes. Then you'll see how annoying it is to be completely irrelevant." I smiled as the wine came, waiting while Hunter tasted the wine and gave his approval.

"You are not completely irrelevant, Olivia, and yes, that would be annoying."

We sipped our wine in silence until I asked, "What's in store for tomorrow?"

"You have the afternoon free again. Do you want to get up with me for breakfast, or order it in your room?"

My eyebrows rose as an excited smile drifted up my face. "I've never had room service! I think I'll do that."

"You'll find that the food isn't as fresh and hot as you might like," Hunter said in distaste.

"Don't care. It's the idea of the thing."

"Here we are." The waitress appeared with a tray and a stand. She set one on the other before serving our meals. The delicious aroma of seared meat made my mouth water. I picked up my knife and fork while Hunter received his plate and wasted no time taking a bite.

"Hunter."

Hearing the voice, we glanced up as Bruce strolled up still wearing the jeans and shirt I had seen him in earlier. He had a book in his hand. "I won't disturb your meal—"

Hunter wiped his mouth and half stood. "Join us."

"No, no. I've just finished. I wanted to say I'll be in the bar, if you and Livy want to stop by for a drink."

"Of course." Hunter remained standing. "Which bar?"

"There's more than one?" Bruce's mouth turned down in a funny-looking frown, but his eyes glittered. He looked at me. "I think they assume businessmen are alcoholics."

"They might be right," I said.

His booming laugh drew eyes around us. He didn't seem to notice as he refocused on Hunter. "The one just off the lobby. That's the only one I knew about."

"There is another, less trafficked bar toward the back of the building. It's quieter, and it's closer to our transportation. If you don't mind, I'd rather not make Livy walk more than she has to. She's trying to break in new shoes, and the effect on her heels is never pretty."

"Of course!" Bruce looked at me in seriousness before glancing under the table. "Oh yeah, those'll wear a hole in your feet for sure! My wife does nothing but complain when she wears a new pair of heels. Why you women put yourselves through it, I'll never know."

"I never used to, but sneakers don't look great with a dress," I said in a light tone.

"Well, that's just an opinion." Bruce leaned down and rubbed my shoulder in jest. "Okay, sure, I'll meet you there. Great catching you—I'm interested in hearing more of your ideas."

"Ask him for a flow chart—he probably has one." I

laughed.

"Right, right." Bruce gave a thumbs-up. "Now sit, sit. Enjoy your dinner. The steak is pretty good." He turned, then flinched as a bustling waitress nearly mowed him down. He apologized and continued on.

"Clever, using me as a scapegoat to get more intimate with him," I said as Hunter retook his seat.

"Intimate doesn't matter—my father will be there, no matter where *there* is." Hunter's eyes hit mine in complete seriousness. "Less walking would be more comfortable for you. I knew Bruce would understand."

I looked down at my food, touched by his concern. To cover the moment, in case he tried to absolve his guilt with another warning about breaking my heart, I said, "Is your father as good at business as you are? You know, the planning and long-term goals and all that?"

"I surpassed the teacher while I was still in school. He's shortsighted and vain. I focus less on short-term gain. It takes longer for my plans to come to fruition, but once they do, I turn heads."

"And you're turning heads now?"

"Yes. Mostly. But I'm not as popular with some of the board members. They want immediate results. It's stunted some things."

"Sounds like an uphill battle."

Hunter reached for his glass with a ghost of a smile. "Yes."

We fell into silence for a moment before I said, "So what's the deal with not smiling? You don't like my jokes?"

A glimmer of sorrow haunted Hunter's gaze. "I fell out of practice, I guess."

"Life can do that. Kick you in the balls."

"Yes," Hunter said again. It was his turn to look down at his food. "It can."

I waited, hoping he'd say a little more. I wanted him to confide in me, to offload some of the pain from his past. I wanted to help him heal. But his gaze stayed downturned as he reached for his glass and took a sip. It was going to fester a while longer.

We finished dinner and paid the check. Hunter was clearly eager to get to Bruce, but he didn't rush me. He waited for my decision on dessert, then asked if I was sure I wanted to turn down the chocolate. I really didn't, but I was doing the right thing. I was getting paid for this trip and I should be putting business before chocolate. It was one of life's cruel jokes.

When everything was squared away, we made our way to the bar.

"Your father might not have found him yet," I said in a supportive tone.

"He has an assistant that watches potential marks pretty closely. He would've tried to catch Bruce at dinner. Failing that, he would've followed soon after Bruce left. I just hope not too much damage has been done."

"Won't it be a little obvious that your father is following him around like a begging dog?"

"He's sly. He's had a lot of experience in this sort of thing."

"I think you give the man too much credit."

We came upon an area with small, circular tables positioned around the floor near a short bar with glittering bottles of alcohol on glass shelves. A man with a white apron and a large belly shook a silver canister behind the bar.

Bruce sat at one of the small tables. Three other white bucket seats surrounded the table, one of them occupied by Hunter's nemesis.

"I will say that's it's scary how well you know your dad," I murmured.

"He taught me his tactics. He wasn't impressed when I called them unethical and refused to follow his teaching."

The hairs stood up on my arms with the viciousness in Hunter's voice, and the harshness of his tone. We walked up to the table, me smiling, Hunter doing his customary blank face.

Bruce glanced up with a troubled expression. Upon recognizing us, he stood and put out his hand. "Sit, please. I guess I don't have to ask if you know Rodge."

Rodge laughed good-naturedly. He made no move to leave. Instead, he rested his hand on the back of the chair next to him. "Please, have a seat, Olivia. It's nice to see you again."

His slimy voice curdled my smile. I stepped back as if the chair was on fire. "I'll just get a round of drinks, shall

I?"

"Of course not. Sit here," Hunter said in his commanding voice, pulling out the seat next to Bruce.

I scurried over and took the seat gratefully, noticing Rodge's hand slowly slide off the top of the seat as his eyes turned hard. A predatory smile graced his face as he ticked his head in a "whatever you wish" sort of way.

"What can I get everyone?" Hunter hadn't dropped the roughness from his voice.

"They have a cute little waitress that comes around," Rodge said easily, crossing a leg over his ankle. "Sit, son. Join us. We were just discussing why I wouldn't lay anyone off if I was granted the buyout."

Hunter sat without expression. He glanced at me. "Do you need anything?"

"I'll just wait for a drink."

"Yes, talking business in front of disinterested parties would be incredibly boring." Bruce turned in his seat and put a finger in the air. The waitress bustled over immediately.

"I'll have another." Bruce held up his empty glass.

Rodge tapped his glass and gave the woman a wink.

"Another?" She nodded at him, answering her own question. Her attention turned to Hunter. He looked at me.

"Do you have Blue Moon?" I asked.

"Blue Moon?" She nodded at me before looking back at Hunter again. She'd answered her own question again.

"Your best scotch, neat," Hunter said.

"Please," I muttered.

"What's that?" Bruce asked as the woman moved away, leaning toward me.

"Oh." I bit my lip before allowing a sheepish smile. "Just finishing Hunter's sentence. You know…the social etiquette thing…" I scratched my cheek to put a barrier between Hunter's eyes and my red face.

Bruce's booming laugh rocketed out across the mostly empty bar area.

"My son has never had great manners," Rodge said with laughter in his voice.

As Hunter's expression darkened, I waved Rodge away. "Not at all. The man is a first-grade gentleman in most things. He's the only man who's ever stood when I got up, or pulled my chair out and waited until I sat. That's old school, right there. He's just used to giving orders." I leaned back as the waitress came back with drinks. "Just have to get used to it. Everyone has their quirks."

"That is true." Bruce took his beer from the waitress. She put the rest of the drinks on the table and wandered away.

"So how have you found the lectures so far?" Bruce asked Hunter.

Hunter reached for his scotch unhurriedly. "For a beginner, perhaps they have some value. But I find some of the theories rather limiting."

"You haven't learned anything, then?" Rodge asked with a straight face. His eyes glimmered as he swirled his whisky lazily. The ice cube clinked off the sides of the glass as it swam around. He hid the tension with his son surprisingly easily.

Hunter's jaw tightened. Clearly he found hiding the tension more difficult. "No, and I doubt you did either. Hopefully the topics will prove more interesting tomorrow. You were smart for missing a few, Bruce." Hunter took a sip and put his glass back on the table.

"Yes. I got to work on my hobby without my wife nagging that I need to get out of my office." Bruce nodded at me. "Did you update?"

"Yeah. But, honestly, I didn't see any difference."

"It was more the early levels. You're almost finished with the game. Smart girl."

Rodge leaned forward with just the trace of a smile, his eyes taking on that predatory quality again. Clearly he didn't like being left out of a conversation. I had no doubt he'd try to interrupt as soon as he could. People like him weren't happy unless they were dominating the conversation. If they weren't talking at you, they were talking over you.

Polite me would've tried to include everyone, but this was business. I needed to keep Bruce's focus. Besides, Rodge sucked. I loved having an excuse to verbally spit in his eye.

"I told you, I need to shut off from time to time," I said to Bruce. "And I can program, too. I can see how you set the game up, to some extent. I've learned your rules, so now it's just a matter of exploiting them."

"You cheat!" Bruce pointed at me with a beaming smile.

"I analyze," I corrected.

"She'd be great in business," Rodge said, leaning closer to Bruce. "If only I'd found her first."

Bruce didn't acknowledge him. His eyes had taken on that focused gaze that meant he was thinking about his hobby. "You're right in the middle of my age demographic. I would love your insight on a new game I'm designing. Especially because, right now, it's geared more toward men. My daughter hates it. Maybe you can help me with content, and then proof the bugs that always crop up…"

"Oh, that's right—she's in computers, correct, Olivia?" Rodge asked. He tried to catch my eye. "You went to Stanford, didn't you?"

With some effort, I ignored the direct question. I didn't even glance in Rodge's direction. Focusing solely on Bruce, I said, "Yeah, sure, if you want. I don't have oodles of time, but I should definitely get a hobby. It would be nice to use my education."

"Stanford, huh?" Bruce nodded, a gleam to his eyes. "Yes. This could work."

"What I have for you tomorrow can wait, Livy," Hunter said in a non-concerned tone. "You'll have plenty of time to speak with Bruce."

"That'd be fun to sit in on," Rodge tried again, leaning way forward in his chair.

In contrast, Hunter leaned way back, crossing his

ankle over his knee. Utterly relaxed. He was letting me lead.

Bruce snatched his phone off the table and started pecking at the screen. "I have a couple-hour stretch." He glanced at me in excitement, like a kid discussing building a tree house. "Give me your room number and I'll call you tomorrow."

"Okay. If it gets me out of work, I'm all in." I laughed and sipped my drink.

Bruce winked at Hunter. "I'll owe you one."

"Well, it's not like Hunter will be particularly put out." Rodge laughed good-naturedly. "She's just an admin, after all. Lovely to have around, but not really integral to the business."

Rodge had progressed to using cheap shots now, had he? He thought I was useless as well as worthless?

Ordinarily I'd roll my eyes. I didn't care what a man like him thought. Especially since his admins *were* probably useless. They were probably pretty, dumb, and eager. He probably paid them next to nothing, too. But if playing the wounded dove got Rodge a sour look, I'd ham it up.

I let the smile melt from my face. Lowering my eyes, I picked at my nail, trying to portray how bad that comment stung. *Woe is me, I'm just a lowly admin.*

Glancing up through my eyelashes to see if they were buying it would definitely blow my cover. Instead, I tucked a lock of hair behind my ear and hunched my shoulders. I leaned toward Hunter and quietly said, "I think I'll hit the ladies' room."

He stood immediately and pulled back my chair so I could get out. I felt his hand slide down my back as I moved away.

It was irritating that I had to let Rodge think he had got the upper hand. I hated showing him my vulnerability, even just pretending. But if Bruce grew even a little indignant on my behalf, it'd be worth it. Tarnishing Rodge's character would be the first step toward victory. Hunter and I *had* to beat that snake of a man.

After I washed up, I made my way back out to the table. I noticed Hunter's vacant seat right away. I also saw that Bruce sat rigid, looking at his beer. Rodge was smiling and chatting as if nothing had happened.

Both men glanced up when I returned.

"Ah, you're back." Rodge beamed up at me. "It's much more dismal when all the beauty leaves."

I gave him a placating smile before asking Bruce, "Speaking of beauty—where's Hunter?"

"Here." That velvety voice made me shiver as Hunter came around me. He didn't place his hand on my back, but his eyes delved into me, connecting intimately. "Did you want to head back?"

In confusion, I looked at my beer level. It was still half full. His scotch was, too. I frowned. "Can't leave fallen soldiers behind." I met his concerned eyes again and lowered my voice so the others wouldn't hear. "Why? Are you okay?"

"I'm more concerned about you, Olivia," he whispered, turning his body to face me, cutting the other two out. "If you're uncomfortable, we'll leave right now."

It dawned on me that Hunter didn't know I was acting. He didn't know me well enough to know that someone like Rodge wouldn't affect me. Nor did he realize the power of a six-figure salary to a poor girl with a bunch of debt. I'd shovel dirt with a smile on my face for six figures. I'd wander around this place and serve coffee—who cared? There were way worse things. Like living on the streets.

"Oh, no. I'm good. Well, my feet hurt a little, but another beer should cure that issue." I patted him on the shoulder and moved to my seat. He braced his hands on my chair until I was comfortable. Only then did he sit down himself.

"So what would you do with my company, Olivia?" Bruce said with a bright tone as he settled back. His eyes were serious, though.

Maybe I'd hammed it up a little too much...

"I'd probably wander into your IT department and geek out." I laughed and sipped my drink.

"Yes, you probably would. I've spent a lot of time there." Bruce looked out over the bar. "I have a problem. I have three different voices telling me different things about what they would do, but I have no idea what would be best for the employees."

"Well, preserving them, certainly," Rodge said easily, lightly resting a hand on Bruce's chair to make himself known. I couldn't tell if he knew he'd dug himself a hole a moment ago.

Bruce glanced at Rodge with a contemplative expression, giving Rodge the platform he needed. Boy did Rodge take it and run. He leaned back and began a long-winded explanation about how he could keep the employees and their expertise, and still grow the company. He talked on and on, using business jargon and patting himself on the back at every opportunity.

My eyes glazed over in boredom and I signaled the waitress. When she showed up, thankfully Rodge paused in his speech, giving me a moment to say what had come into my head. "Keeping on the extra people would mean a long, boring day for those without anything to do. If I was in that situation, I'd go crazy."

"I can't imagine you'd sing that tune if you were the one losing her job," Rodge said with a condescending smile.

"I live cheaply. I was stressing after college because I didn't have any income, but if I had unemployment, especially with all the extensions the state is granting, I'd survive. I'd rather job-hunt with a free day and money coming in than go to work and hate my whole day."

"Yes, well—"

"What do you think, Hunter?" Bruce interrupted. "You've been awfully quiet."

Hunter didn't so much as shift positions. "I don't have an opinion that you'd want to hear in a bar. A takeover is not a ten-minute debate over just one issue. For example, you have too many people as it is. The extra salary expense is siphoning off what you could be putting into product development. More redundancies in staff means a bigger money pit, not to mention it eats away at morale when you have people walking around half-dead with boredom, as Olivia said.

"No, I wouldn't keep on the extras. I'd offer a healthy package, aiming at the younger crowd who would stick out their hand with a smile and then go blow it in Europe. Then I would focus on breathing new life into your old hobby. The possibilities just five years down the road would excite you, I'm sure. But that will all take time and planning—things hard to express with an opposing viewpoint seated next to me."

"Point proven, decidedly." I widened my eyes and grimaced comically at Bruce over the rim of my glass. I lowered my voice to a stage whisper. "He sure told us."

He laughed and stood. "Yes he did. Food for thought. Well, I need to hit the hay. My mind is whirling from all this business talk."

"Mine is half-dead with boredom," I said with a smile before I sipped my drink.

Bruce said, "Thanks for joining me. I'll see you in the lectures tomorrow." His gaze hit mine. "Which room are you in? I'll call the room tomorrow to see what time you can come geek out with me."

I gave him the number as Hunter stood. He put a hand out to help me up. "We'll head away, too, I think. It's late."

It was barely nine o'clock, but I took a swig and

stood anyway. Without bothering to look at Rodge, the snake, I tucked my hand into Hunter's arm and let him lead me away. We trailed behind Bruce a little and gave a wave when he turned a corner. As we exited the building and found the golf carts, Hunter said, "You're a genius. I hadn't thought about young people who wouldn't mind being laid off. And I bet Bruce hadn't, either. That helps me a great deal, Livy."

I climbed in the passenger side. There was no way I'd find my way back in the dark. "Guys like you don't often think about things like that," I said, as Hunter drove.

He reached across the space between us and gently took my hand. His fingers threaded through mine. "Are you sure you're okay with my father's comment?"

He was holding my hand!

I closed my eyes as the electricity jumped through the contact. I wanted more. I wanted all.

"I was acting, Hunter," I said in a breathy voice. "I don't care about anything he said, and I certainly don't care what your dad thinks. He's too impressed with himself to be worth my time. But I knew it was a dick thing to say, so I thought I'd make sure Bruce noticed it."

Hunter parked and turned to me. The yellow light from the lamp next to us made his features appear as if they were carved in stone by some great master. His hand came up and rested on my chin lightly. His thumb traced my lower lip. I could barely see his eyes in the dim light, staring at my mouth.

"He did. I did," Hunter whispered, bending closer. His lips barely glanced off mine, sending shooting sparks through my body.

I closed my eyes, feeling his breath mingle with mine. Feeling it quicken as he kissed the very edge of my mouth. "I can't ignore how you affect me, Livy," he said quietly. "I want to kiss you so bad it hurts."

"Then kiss me, Hunter. Please."

He pulled my head closer and leaned his forehead against mine. "I…can't. I can't do this."

"Why?"

His hands came to the side of my face. I felt him trembling as his nose slid beside mine, bringing our lips closer again. We breathed the same air, hot and fast, wanting each other. So close.

He exhaled and backed away, regret dragging down his features. "Because I'm screwed up, Olivia." Sorrow infused his tone. "Because I'm badly screwed up, and I'd just drag you down with me. Some people can get over issues in their past. Some people can heal. I'm not one of them."

"What happened to you?"

He turned from me and exited the golf cart. "I was taken for a fool, and it scared me from wanting the things that others want. Come on."

Tingling deep in my core, I followed him without comment. We wound through the corridor until we reached my room. He waited for me to unlock the door before opening it for me. He glanced at the connecting door, which was still closed.

When he looked back at me, fire fueled his gaze. "I want to fuck you, Olivia. But won't if you'd rather not."

His velvety voice licked up my center and stole my breath. I nodded dumbly, my sex still swollen from the golf cart and now pounding furiously.

"Come to me when you're ready."

Chapter 5

HE DOOR CLOSED with a loud click that made me flinch. I turned to my suitcase, since I hadn't put anything in the closet, and pawed through the various sexy items I'd brought. Black silk and lace slid through my fingers. I pulled it out and laid it on the bed before pulling out a garter as well.

The material whispered as it fell over my skin. The end stopped on my upper thigh, revealing the garter. Lace dipped low on my neckline, showing right up to my nipples before the silk took over. I slipped into red high heels before opening the inner door.

Hunter sat on his couch without a shirt. His perfectly cut upper body drew my gaze and made my mouth water. I entered his room before making a decision on location. I walked straight to the bed and pulled back the covers. I crawled to the center on all fours before I remembered his conversation earlier. He didn't spend the night. He didn't cuddle.

I didn't want to be kicked out. I'd rather him leave

when I was already asleep. No harm, no foul.

Kind of.

I backed out as he stood. As I moved back to my room, he met my eyes. I didn't bother saying a word, just walked through the door. A flash of regret crossed his face. He knew what I was doing, and why.

I didn't let it affect me. I needed his body against mine. I needed him inside me. If I had to go to bed alone, I'd do nothing but think of him. I didn't care how deeply I was in—I was beyond being able to deny myself.

I lay down on my bed and flared out my hair, settling into a sexy pose as he entered. All he wore were silk boxers, having removed the rest of his clothes before stepping into my space. He approached the bed like an animal sensing prey. His eyes burned as they devoured my body.

He moved onto the bed until his side was pressed up against me. His hand ran over my stomach, feeling the material, before moving up, over the swell of my breast.

"You're so beautiful." His lips trailed along my jaw. He reached between my thighs, nudging them wider before moving the material away from my bare sex.

His breath grew heavy as his fingers trailed up my wet slit before circling the top lazily. One finger dipped into my body.

My breath hitched and my body arched. I spread my legs wider. Another finger joined the first as he lightly sucked on the fevered skin of my neck. His fingers plunged, making me grab for him.

His mouth moved down my chest. He pulled lace to the side, revealing my breast before sucking in a constricted nipple. I gave a strangled moan as his fingers moved more rapidly. Pleasure unfurled and moved through my body. I arched again, running my fingers through his hair.

He lifted my nightie and then kissed down my stomach, circling my navel with his tongue. His big body moved between my legs, sinking until I felt his hot mouth on my core. I cried out, arching up.

His fingers worked faster as his tongue swirled, firing shocks of intense desire through me. Pleasure wound through my body, tightened me up. I shivered and gyrated my hips up wildly. My muscles flexed. My breathing turned ragged. "Oh… Oh G… *Oh*—"

An orgasm rocked through me. I convulsed in ecstasy, squeezing my eyes shut as my body shuddered within the waves of pleasure.

"Holy moly," I said in a breathy voice as all my muscles began to relax. "That was good."

Hunter moved up quickly, not giving me long to revel. He pushed his briefs down and then off. His fingers wrapped around the base of his cock and moved his tip from the bottom to the top of my wetness. He positioned at my opening before laying his body fully on mine. He licked and bit up my neck as he pushed forward.

"Ooooh." I sighed as he filled me. My eyes fluttered as I stretched around him, so deliciously full.

Pleasure started battering me almost immediately. I scratched up his back and squeezed his middle with my thighs. His thick length moved within me. My hips swung up to him, taking him deep. With panting breath, I pushed his face up until his lips hovered just above mine. I could feel the heat of his breath and the roll of his body.

My hands trailed down his broad back to his butt. I gripped harder, pulling him into me as my hips pushed up to meet him.

"Yes, Olivia," he growled, pounding into me. He hit off me with a wet smack, the sounds of sex filling the room.

"Mmmm, *harder*," I said, closing my eyes.

His body rocked into me with more force. So deep. So filling.

I hugged him close as he labored. "Yes, Hunter," I said, rocking up.

"Livy..." His voice coated me with longing. With both passion and pleasure, but also with a feeling deeper than I'd heard in his voice before. More substantial.

I opened my eyes to see him looking down on me, his eyes liquid brown in the dim light. His gaze settled on my lips as fear covered his face, but still he bent toward me, barely glancing his lips off mine. "Livy..." His emotion showed in his eyes, in his deep, passionate thrusts, making it impossible for me to speak.

I rose, trying to capture his kiss. Trying to cross the barrier that terrified him. Wanting to protect him with love and support.

He hugged me tightly as his movements got smaller, but infinitely more potent. His lips glanced off mine again but still didn't connect. His tongue came out and licked my bottom lip.

I moaned, everything so tight. The movements so intense. I couldn't breathe. I couldn't speak.

With his next powerful thrust, I shattered. A swell of pleasure pulled me under. I clutched Hunter, squeezing him close as I cried my release. He shook a moment later, groaning.

The sound of our labored breath filled the room. One by one, my muscles relaxed, and then melted. I closed my eyes, content with his weight and warmth on top of me. With his body still inside me.

He shifted and kissed my cheek tenderly. He moved to the side, turning me to face away from him before curling up behind. His arms still hugged me close. My back pressed into his hard chest.

I slipped my hand into his and settled more firmly into the pillow. I knew he'd wait until I fell asleep, and that my back would be cold when I woke in the morning. But I did not regret these times with him. Not for one moment. He kept saying he couldn't love, but each time we were together was more intense. More passionate. He gave in just that little bit more. I just needed to be patient.

Chapter 6

T HE PHONE IN my room rang. I paused with my brush caught in my hair and dashed over. "Hello?"

"Olivia, this is Bruce."

"Oh hey." I yanked on the brush, wincing as my head yanked with it.

"I was thinking about heading to the lagoon in a while, if you'd still like to join me?"

"Yeah, sure. You know, there's a spot closer to the hotel that has better Wi-Fi, if you'd rather go there?"

"Great. Where?"

I explained the location to Bruce, a place Hunter had found and texted me about an hour before. Bruce confirmed we'd meet in half an hour before hanging up.

I yanked at my brush again, trying to dislodge it. My hair was a rat's nest from all the rolling around I'd done with Hunter last night.

My heart warmed at the thought.

He'd lain with me until I'd fallen asleep, as I'd expected. What I hadn't expected was waking up in the small hours of the morning as he slipped his arm out from under me before quietly making his way back to his own room. I wasn't sure if it was another compromise, that he'd loaned his body heat and comfort to reduce the sting of his father from earlier, or if he'd stayed for his own benefit.

One explanation made more sense than the other, but hope was a dangerous thing. I chose not to think about it much. It was safer that way.

I threw on a sweater and took to my hair again, working the tangles out one by one, another lesson in patience. That done, I slipped into my sneakers and grabbed my computer. Hunter said I was to devote as much time to Bruce as needed. He was my sole focus. If Bruce wanted to blow off work and stick our toes in the lagoon while drinking margaritas, my job was to say, "Absolutely." As Bruce was a really cool guy, I wouldn't be at all put out if he did!

With a bounce in my step, I pushed through the door of the building, headed to my trusty sidekick, the golf cart. As I turned the corner, I bumped into a tall, robust man.

"Oh, sorry," I muttered, stepping to the side to clear the way.

"Not at all." Rodge smiled down at me, a look that had probably knocked women out when he was younger.

"Excuse me," I said, skirting by him.

"You're going to meet Bruce, I take it?" Rodge stepped with me, shadowing me to the empty space where my golf cart should've been.

I glanced around, seeing not just the absence of my golf cart, but of *all* the golf carts.

"They must've cleaned up. Here, I'll walk you," Rodge said, holding his hand out to the right.

I started walking left. "No thanks."

"Hunter is putting a lot of faith in you," Rodge said as he followed me.

"I can make it on my own, Rodge. I don't need an escort."

"No, it doesn't seem you do." His voice dropped an octave, taking on a rougher tone I hadn't heard him use before. "You've done just fine moving in on my man. What you need is a roadblock."

Invisible ants crawled up my spine. That sounded like a threat.

I started walking a little faster, glancing down at my map.

"I've worked very hard on Donnelley, Olivia. Very hard. And in one night—*one* night—you unraveled everything I've meticulously put together. It's disappointing."

"Hunter's a smart man. He knows your tricks, and he's combating them with a more effective method."

"You think you know Hunter, do you?" He chuckled, a dark, grating sound. "No one knows my son like I do. He'll cut out the throats of those closest to him to get what he wants. You think he's letting you learn a new hobby right now? He's not. He's using you to get this mark. After that, he'll return to just using you for sex. Not that I blame him. I'll bet you're a wild little thing..."

I clutched my computer bag a little tighter. "He was completely honest about the situation with Bruce. You're not telling me anything I don't know."

"I see. You like being used, do you? It turns you on. Then maybe you should try the man who created the boy..." Rodge put a firm hand on my shoulder.

Small arms of fear wrapped around my middle. I shrugged him off, fighting panic.

He won't do anything. He's trying to scare you, Olivia. He's trying to get under your skin.

It was working.

"I'm not going to lose this deal to a sniveling little boy, Olivia," Rodge continued in that rough, low voice, walking so close to me that his side brushed mine. "I can make it worth your while. Name your price."

"I'm not for sale."

"Aren't you? Then you let my son treat you like a prostitute for free?"

I recalled Hunter's continued warnings that he wouldn't love me. That I shouldn't care for him, because he wouldn't return the affection. Part of me wondered if what Rodge implied was at least partially true. And I hated myself for even considering it.

"I'll let you think that over," Rodge said, slowing.

His presence drifted away as I walked around a bend. Practically running, I looked around to make sure I was alone, and then staggered into a cluster of trees. Leaning against the bark, I took deep, sob-choked breaths, trying to calm down. Working to erase that smooth, taunting voice from my head.

I knew what I was doing with Hunter. I knew why I'd given him a chance, and it wasn't trading skin for money. It *was* different. He'd broken his protocol for me—he hadn't made me sign that contract in the end. That had to count for something.

So why did I feel so gross?

I wiped away the angry, self-despising tears and composed myself. Rodge was good at getting under people's skin. I couldn't let him win by doing it to me.

I put on a blasé mask and walked into the area housing the man-made lagoon that looked just like the one I had sat beside yesterday. Bruce was sitting at a table near the water with an array of papers spread out in front of him.

"Hey, I was just—" Bruce cut off as his eyes scanned my face. "You okay?"

"Yeah." I shrugged off my bag and turned my face down. Obviously the mask wasn't a great one.

"If Hunter gave you grief about doing this, we can schedule—"

"No, no." I waved him away as I pulled out my computer. "Hunter's fine. I just ran into Rodge. He's...less than thrilled I'm taking face time away from his favorite client."

I laughed, playing it off like a joke as I brought out

my phone. "This is a nice place."

Bruce glanced around before returning his gaze to my face. Concern had his brow furrowing, but he didn't push. Instead, he nodded and said, "Yeah. I thought you'd picked it out. Women are always drawn to pretty things. Or so my wife says, at any rate."

I smiled, letting his unassuming company clear away the dark places Rodge had brought out in me. "Pretty and shiny. Remember that when you need to get her a present."

"Oh yeah. After twenty-five years of marriage, I've learned that lesson."

He grabbed a piece of paper from the table and flung it in my direction. "That's what I was thinking."

And just like that, his extreme focus took over. He'd just switched to work mode.

I laughed, grabbing the piece of paper. Several screen shots of a battle scene were displayed with various combat men pointing guns at each other.

"What?" Bruce asked, looking over the other pages.

"If I wasn't used to Hunter, your sudden mood shift would be jarring."

"Oh." Bruce scoffed. "Yeah, that's a personality flaw. I take some getting used to."

I looked over the images and corresponding notes. I glanced at the other sketches littering the table, trying to work out what he was suggesting. "This is some sort of war game, right?"

"I'm torn between snipers and shoot 'em up."

"You're not going to pull in a whole lot of females, that's for sure. This is a male-dominated category."

Bruce tossed another page at me, this one a pie chart. Market research, I'd bet. "Big money possibilities, though."

"Yes, without a doubt. If you do this right, you could have a very lucrative hobby."

"Lots of competition…" Bruce drummed his fingers.

"Lots. Lots and lots." I laid down the paper. "But what doesn't? Puzzle games do, arcade—they are big categories for a reason. Trying anything new would need even more marketing."

"So put out a cash cow now, and try to invent something new when we have some funds built up…" Bruce kept drumming his fingers as he looked at his notes.

"We, huh?" I smiled, looking over a printout of some of his scripts. "I'm a partner now, am I?"

"Yup. Two people working together go way faster than just one. Besides, once I've sold my company, I'll have a way of getting out of boring conversations."

I gave him a confused look. He grinned. "I'll have to take your *very* important calls."

I barked out a laugh. "Got it." I pushed my computer to the side and glanced at his. "Okay, let's see what ya got."

As soon as he started talking about his ideas, and how he was trying to go about them, it was as if I'd known him all my life. We just clicked. Two hours passed that seemed like ten minutes. We worked off each other easily, each job taking less than half the time it would have done alone. I was having so much fun that when his phone beeped, I very nearly hoped he'd just silence it so we could keep going.

"Back to the grindstone," Bruce said with a sigh, turning off his alarm.

I gave a sound like a whine, probably reminding him of my age. In response, he chuckled as he gathered up his notes.

"Why are you here, if you're selling your business?" I asked, saving and closing out of my programs. I'd have to go back to the endless stream of emails now, looking at things Hunter wanted me to know that were way above my pay grade.

"Truthfully, I wanted to understand the best way to go about business so that I might be able to handle this hobby without losing control like I did of the other one."

"Your other business just blew up?"

Bruce packed his computer away. "Almost overnight, yes. I just started hiring people and shoved work at them, trying to keep up with demand. Everything just…got way out of control. Way over my head."

"I hear that." I leaned my elbows on the table, watching him get ready to go to his next meeting.

When he was done, he turned straight to me and said, "Tell me the truth—is the Hunter Carlisle I saw last night legit, or is he putting on a persona to gain my business?"

I didn't even hesitate. "That's him. A jerk with a

'please' problem, but genuine. He's always taken care of those around him. I told you that when I first met you."

Bruce's expression turned incredulous. "I wouldn't have thought it. I thought he was a hard-ass, excuse my language. Only in it for himself. The arrogant way he goes about explaining himself just rubs me wrong. I thought he'd tear down everything I built to rip out a few gold nuggets to add to his coffers."

"He might," I said in all seriousness. "It's got nothing to do with you, but he's obsessed with efficiency and productivity—if something isn't working, he'll tear it down and rebuild. He'll make your company shine in the long run, but first he'll completely reshape it to make it fit in his company. I've heard enough stories around the office to know that he is a genius when it comes to that sort of thing. That's why he has his job. And keeps his job. But yeah, he can be a dick. No two ways about it."

Bruce barked out laughter. "Your honesty is refreshing. With the way he looked after you last night, I saw a different man than the one I've met in the past. Completely different. Made me think a little harder about what he was saying."

"Preaching to the choir. His driver wanted to punch him in the face a few times. But he's still there and happy as a clam."

Bruce tilted his head in that way people did when they resigned themselves to a different way of thinking. "You oughta know."

"Yep." I pulled my computer back in front of me.

"I'll email you all our notes with a list of things we can tackle immediately before we plan the next leg."

"Please remember that when you find yourself with entire days to fill, I'll still have a fifty- to sixty-hour-a-week job…"

He shouldered his computer bag. "No promises."

I opened my first email and groaned immediately. "Hunter, give me a break!"

Bruce's laugh boomed as he walked away.

Chapter 7

HUNTER AND I found ourselves at a Thai restaurant at the far corner of the hotel complex. The food was much better than the steakhouse, but had very few diners. It seemed all the businessmen wanted steak, regardless of quality, and that was that.

We'd talked about nothing much since he picked me up from my room. I'd had the connecting door closed again, needing some time to reflect. As much as I hated to admit it, Rodge had affected me. I needed to reaffirm what I was doing with Hunter, and that required talking to myself. I really didn't need Hunter overhearing my rambling. Especially when it was about him.

Hunter laid down his chopsticks after he'd cleared his plate and looked at me with heavy, delving eyes. "Bruce mentioned you'd been speaking to my father."

Suspicion rang in his voice. It seemed I wasn't the only one affected by Rodge.

"Yes. All the golf carts were gone. I had to walk to meet Bruce, and Rodge was right there to take advantage of it."

"What did you talk about?"

My stomach turned, both because of my doubt, and because of the way Hunter was interrogating me.

There goes my appetite. I put my chopsticks down and pushed my plate away. "He knows you use your admins for sex, and came to the conclusion that I'm happy being used." Heat prickled my eyes, threatening tears. I bit my lip and looked away, trying to hold back the emotion that had been threatening me all day. "Who knows. Maybe I am. It's better than the alternative."

Hunter's voice softened. "Which is?"

"That I let you use me for money." Tears flooded my eyes. "He offered to buy me. Since you had. I felt about *this* small." I offered up my thumb and index finger to demonstrate before looking away.

Hunter stood and came around the table. He pulled me up and quickly walked us from the restaurant. On the way out, he told the hostess his name and room and said to bill the dinner. We turned to the right and pushed out through an exit. The chill of the night brushed my face, helping to dry the streaks of tears. Hunter shrugged out of his jacket and draped it across my shoulders as he led us to a bench secluded in darkness.

"You were willing to try the job for a month without the stipulation of sex," Hunter said in a soft and smooth voice. He put his arm over my shoulder and drew me into his side. "I wasn't supposed to touch you, remember? And I tried not to. I really did. Every day I had to hold myself back. But then you wore that sexy outfit, and you were so close—I touched you before I knew what I was doing. It wasn't because you offered yourself; it was because I pushed myself on you.

"You have to remember—my father manipulates. That's what he does. He must know you can't be bought, or he'd be working that angle with all his charm. Instead, he's making you feel like…this. Like someone of little worth and moral value. He knows exactly what he's doing here, Olivia. You aren't the girl he's trying to say you are."

"I signed the contract."

"It wasn't because of the sex. We both know that. I know the sort of person you are, Livy, which is why I give you the warnings I do when the guilt starts to eat away at me. I'm the monster here, not you. I'm the one preying on you, not the other way around."

"You're not preying on me," I murmured, burrowing into him.

His arms tightened around me until he moved me onto his lap and hugged me into his chest. He put my arms around his shoulders and rested my face against his neck. He said, "Some women take my father up on his offers. His second wife, for a start. And his third. His fourth will, too, whoever she turns out to be. She'll be half his age and less than that in IQ, and she'll give up happiness for his bank account. I knew you wouldn't— in my heart, I knew. I *know,* I should say. But old wounds make it hard not to question. I shouldn't have accused you like I did. I'm sorry."

I breathed in his smell, letting him hold me. His strong arms felt so secure. His apology so heartfelt.

"Are you okay?" he asked softly, giving me a lingering kiss on my cheek.

"As good as can be expected from being pitted between you and your dad."

Hunter kissed me again, letting his lips remain on my skin for a while before squeezing me again. "You put up with a lot from me."

I was pretty sure I brought most of it on myself, but I didn't want to argue. Instead, I said, "Let's get a drink."

"Of course. Should we go back for your jacket?"

"Why, are you getting cold?"

"I don't get cold—I'm a man." He stood with me in his arms before he bent to place me delicately on the ground.

"You'd probably repeat that over and over until you froze to death."

"Probably."

I leaned against his side, feeling the pressure of his hand on the small of my back. "I am sorry about my father," he said as we reached the door.

"He tried to say you were using me to get at Bruce. If you hadn't been honest about that, I would've been thrown for a loop."

"Any other admin and I wouldn't have mentioned it. I trust you. I trust that you see what I'm trying to do, and are as invested in the cause as I am. I don't know why my father just won't let things lie. He constantly turns up in my life to cause havoc."

We stopped along the way to get my jacket before moving on to a different restaurant. This one was Japanese and advertised karaoke on Friday and Saturday nights. Thankfully, it was Thursday, which meant the dance floor was clear of bad singers. The mellow sounds of a string quartet played over the sound system.

Hunter led me into the bar, a sectioned-off area with full access to the dance floor. We sat at one of the tables amid half a dozen businessmen and waited for the waitress to work around to us.

"So you talked to Bruce…" I started as Hunter leaned back in his seat and stretched out his legs.

"Yes. He approached me, actually. First, he raved about you. Warned me that if he wasn't selling his company, he'd steal you away to work for him."

"I'm sure he's got a bunch of programmers way better than me."

Hunter's lips quirked, almost a grin. "Probably, but they are probably all geeky men who spent their youths in their mothers' basements playing video games. They aren't Bruce's speed. Or so he said, when I told him exactly what you did."

"Oh ye of little faith," I huffed, quieting when the waitress came for our orders. "I may be from the working class, but I haven't actually *worked,*" I continued after we'd given them.

"You have a good work ethic. That goes a long way. And you're fun. If it wasn't for you, he would never have sought me out. If not for you, I would be lost."

The music was turned up and lights dimmed. The disco ball in the center of the floor started spinning, catching and throwing the lights in a way that offset the subtle sounds of the string quartet.

I pushed the hair away from my eyes with the back of my hand. It was a little *Gone with the Wind,* but my heart was fluttering with what he'd said, and, more importantly, the tone he said it in. "If I wasn't here, would you have hounded him a bit more?" I said.

Hunter sipped his drink. "I wouldn't have had a chance. My father had all but sold him. But with you— you stand out. When we were all together, the four of us, I saw it immediately. I figured stepping back and letting your unassuming charm come through was the best way to play it."

I was two seconds from fanning my face and fainting. I needed to get a grip! "And your father…"

"Doesn't think anyone can do his job better than him. It's why his company is bottlenecked right now. It's as big as it'll ever get with him in charge—any larger and he'd have to give up some precious control."

"I always thought you were controlling."

"I can be in certain situations…" His eyes glimmered with heat. My heartbeat increased. He leaned forward and extended a hand. "May I have this dance?"

"Wha—" I glanced around the bar, suddenly embarrassed. That was *not* where I thought he was going with the heat infusing his eyes. "Uh… I can certainly shake a leg, but ballroom dancing isn't in my repertoire."

"C'mon, Livy." He stood, reaching down to take my hand.

"No one is out there! We'll stand out. But not in a good way!"

"Just follow my lead." He led me to the dance floor and turned me toward him, waiting for me to rest my hand on his shoulder. He brought my other hand in close, resting our hands against his chest.

I sighed as he stepped forward, making me step backward with him. I felt the soft music drifting down around us as the light from the disco ball showered us. His grip tightened further and his steps became shorter, allowing for more contact between us. His cheek came in close to my face. His heat enveloped me along with his delicious smell.

"See?" he whispered in my ear. "Nothing to it."

I closed my eyes and exhaled as I felt his body moving. His strong and sure lead left no doubt about his intentions within the dance, and as long as I matched those movements, and let my body melt into his, I had no problem keeping up. His heart beat steadily against our held hands. His lips softly glanced against my face, leading to the corner of my mouth. He stopped there and backed away, looking down on me.

Hunger infused his gaze, but there was also a softness I hadn't been expecting. "I didn't really need you to come on this trip."

I stared at his lips, desperate to be kissed. Wanting to feel the electricity from the contact. "I thought you wanted me to make contact with Bruce."

"I did, but that wasn't the real reason I brought you."

"And what was?" I asked in a breathy whisper. His mouth dipped toward mine. Longing infused his eyes.

He winced, glancing down at his side. He reached down to his pocket before taking out his phone. "Bruce wants to speak with me. Privately."

There were many things I probably should've said, like "Exciting!" Or "That's promising." Instead, I uttered a disappointed "Oh."

It wasn't the most professional of responses.

He looked at me for a long moment. "I'm sorry. I have to go."

"Yeah! Of course you do." I followed him back to the table. "I'll just head back. I'm tired, anyway."

"I think he wants to talk business." I could see the regret in his eyes. "It might be a while. I most likely won't see you tonight…"

"Hunter, you're not a sex dispenser. Relax. But I'm taking my beer with me."

He gave a small smile. The action had me stopping as I reached for my glass and staring.

His face transformed from extremely handsome to something indescribable. His eyes shone from within, infusing me until I felt a smile build in response. He was hotter than any model, and more charismatic than any celebrity. And that was just with the smallest of grins. I couldn't imagine what a whole smile would do. Probably melt my panties.

"Sounds fair." His thumbs flew across his phone before he slipped it back into his pocket. He peeled off a bill from a thick money roll and handed it to the waitress when she came around.

"I'll just get your change," she said, diving into her pockets.

"No need." He put his hand on the small of my back and waited for me to step out in front of him.

"Are you sure?"

Hunter ignored her as he escorted me out. We were followed with a "Thank you!"

"You are so incredibly rude while being over-the-top generous. How do you pull that off?" I said as we made it outside and Hunter chose a golf cart.

"It's a gift."

"From a white elephant party, maybe."

He handed me into the golf cart before walking to the other side and climbing in. "I overheard someone giving the staff an earful about having no carts at his disposal," he said, as he started the engine. "He did not like having to walk."

"Was he in our building?"

"Yes. And the staff said that they only re-park the carts, but that there are always carts available unless they've all been used."

A sickening feeling came over me. "Would Rodge

have moved the carts?"

"He doesn't necessarily subscribe to ethics…"

"What a…" I stopped there. I had a few names I could use, and none of them were very ladylike.

We parked in front of our building, where the golf carts were once again in a line. Hunter escorted me to my room even though I protested I could get there just fine on my own. As I opened the door, I turned back to him.

"Knock 'em dead." I smiled at him.

His eyes were serious as he beheld me. He stared for a long moment before turning around and walking the way we had come.

"Okay, *goodbye*…" I muttered as I closed the door. "Manners, anyone?"

I went to my suitcase and pulled out a few silky things, but then grabbed my oversized T-shirt. If he planned to be wheeling and dealing late into the night, he wouldn't come in and wake me. I was hopefully safe in comfortable yet frumpy attire.

Chapter 8

━━━∾∾∾━━━

I CAME AWAKE slowly. It took me a moment to realize what woke me up. I glanced at the clock. It was just after midnight.

Another soft rap came from the connecting door. Hunter wanted to see me.

With a thrill of excitement, I threw back the covers and lurched toward the door. Yawning, I undid the latch and then stretched my arms, trying to chase away the stiffness from deep sleep. I'd forgotten that the door was closed. I hadn't figured he'd want to connect with me tonight, so didn't worry about it.

I pulled open the door, shivering with the cold. Not seeing anyone, I peeked inside his room, catching him coming around the corner from the restroom, shirtless.

"Hunter?"

"Sorry—I didn't mean to wake you. I—" He cut off as his gaze hit me. It traveled my face, to my hair, and then down to the YMCA T-shirt that hung loosely off my frame.

There was absolutely no way I could look less sexy than I did right then. I probably should've thought of that before I opened the door…

"Uh…" I crossed my arms. "I, ah…I didn't dress up. I can go put something else on, if you want?"

He walked to me slowly, as if in a daze. His eyes came to rest on mine. "Bruce is going with me. He listened to my whole plan, cuts included, and where I think I can be in five years. I told him what would happen if we didn't go with him, too, and what I thought about that. He gave me an unofficial nod. You did it."

"*You* did it—I just got you a meeting and an open mind."

Fire burned in his gaze. He stepped closer, inches from me now. His tone should've been excited, or happy, or filled with pride, but instead, it was dripping with desire.

I gulped loudly. My nipples constricted under the heat of that stare, poking the silly shirt I wore.

He noticed. His hand came around me and pulled me into his body. "You are so damn sexy, Olivia. So, so beautiful."

Possibly he hadn't noticed the shirt. Somehow. "I didn't think I'd see you."

"I should've let you sleep. But…" His expression grew troubled. "I missed you tonight. I wanted to share the good news."

His hand came up to my chin and lifted my face. His

eyes focused on my lips. "I need your presence, Olivia. It's all I can think about when you're not around. You're all I can think about." He shook his head as his frown deepened. "I don't know myself anymore."

His head bent. Uncertainty flashed across his expression. "But I can't ignore this. Not anymore." His lips glanced across mine once, before he steadied. His lips connected with mine. He opened my mouth with his while tilting his head, deepening the contact. His tongue flitted into my mouth. He was giving in!

A pure shot of electricity coursed through my body and singed my insides. Goosebumps spread across my skin as shivers racked me. My head went dizzy and my sex throbbed. I moaned into his mouth with fluttering eyes, running my hands up his chest and losing myself in his sweet yet wild taste.

"I want to make love to you, Livy," he mumbled against my lips.

My breath caught. I almost didn't believe the word he'd used instead of *fuck*. "Yes, Hunter."

He didn't push me into my room; he pulled me into his. The door shut with a soft click before he bent down and scooped me up into his arms. His lips connected with mine again. Bursts of pleasure exploded in my body with the feel of his lips. With the heat of his body. With the fact that he was ignoring his fears and giving in. To me.

He set me down long enough to strip off my T-shirt and his pants before laying me in the center of the bed.

Without a word, he settled himself between my thighs, resting his body on top of mine. His kiss deepened. Became more passionate. He threaded his fingers through mine as his hips slowly pushed toward me, sending his manhood deep into my body.

"I've wanted this since the beginning, Livy," he murmured against my lips.

I fell into the sensations. Holding on to his words. My body wound tighter, and then tighter still, as he thrust into me, over and over. I whimpered as the pleasure shook me in waves. His tongue flicked in my mouth, needy and insistent, mimicking our lovemaking. My eyes fluttered with the feel of him. His hard length inside, his solid body on top.

"Mmm," I moaned, tightening my legs around him. Electricity surged, his kiss applying the final ingredient to an already addictive recipe. "Yes, Hunter."

I gyrated my hips, meeting his thrusts. He crashed into me. My moaning grew louder. His kisses became fervent, almost desperate. I matched his intensity, letting it all go. All control, all hope of keeping a part of myself from him—I opened up fully for him to take.

Without warning, pleasure like I'd never experienced flooded into my body. I convulsed, crying out. Ecstasy vibrated up my middle.

Hunter slowed for a moment, his kiss turning languid. My body matched.

And then he started again. Faster now. Whipping my body back into a frenzy.

"Oh, no, Hunter," I said as the feeling once again redlined. Pleasure so sharp it cut. My muscles flexed, my body primed for another orgasm.

He pumped into me, hitting all the right places. His hard chest teased my sensitive nipples. His clever tongue flicked and tasted, taking me higher than he had before.

"Oh, Hunter. Oh…" I tried to take my hands out of his so I could scratch his back, but he wouldn't set me free. He held on, increasing the friction. Moving faster.

Panting, I squeezed him tighter with my thighs. I tried to arch, getting away from that tantalizing kiss. There was just too much. Too much sensation. I was drowning in it.

"I won't make this easy on you, Olivia," he whispered. "Because it's far from easy for me. I want all of you."

"Already…gave…myself."

"I don't want just your body. I want your heart. I want you to give us much as I'm about to."

My stomach flipped. My heart swelled as expectation filled me. Without warning, another climax tore through me. "Oh!"

He nibbled my lips as he let go of my hands. His arms worked around my body as he sat up, pulling me up with him. He wrapped my legs around his waist and felt down my back until his hands were on my hips. He kept me moving over him now, thrusting upward as he brought me down, getting deeper. Taking another little piece of me.

I let my head fall back, moaning. The winding in my core intensified, coiling into a tight ball of unbearable pleasure. "No, please," I said, squeezing my eyes tight against the feelings.

Hunter's fingers curled around the back of my neck and he brought my face into his. His lips claimed mine again. His taste, savory and wild, blossomed in my senses, adding to the feel of his body and the depth of his thrust. "Ohhh God," I groaned as yet another orgasm broke me down.

Still he kept going, faster now, winding again. Pounding my body with exquisite pleasure. Making me writhe and twist over him, unsure if I wanted to run to or away from him. Unsure what this all meant, only that I was too far in now. Too far. I couldn't give any more. He demanded too much.

As if hearing me, he said, "A little bit more, baby. Give me just a little bit more."

He hugged me tighter, almost cutting off my breath. I held on for dear life, digging my nails into him for something to hold on to as everything around me flew apart.

I whimpered with another orgasm, immediately building. "Just a little bit more," he promised, thrusting harder. Pumping into my body with wild abandon. Holding on to me to keep me rooted to him.

"Little…bit…more," he whispered, giving me another deep, body-consuming kiss. Another climax, shuddering me over him, squeezing out a tear.

Raw. I felt completely raw, emotionally and physically. Pushed too far. Broken.

"Good girl." Hunter pushed us forward until we tumbled onto the bed in a mess of limbs.

On overdrive, my hips swung up of their own accord, striving for the big completion all these orgasms had been driving toward. To the final act that would cement what making love was really about.

Hunter's lips were never far from mine, not even to kiss another part of me. Always connected, body and soul. Demanding I stay connected too.

"Almost there," he whispered.

I clung to him in desperation, tears in my eyes, scared and in awe at the same time with what I was giving to another human being. But he held me so tight, protecting me, possessing me. Honoring me.

"Come with me, baby," Hunter commanded, emotion dripping from every word.

His lips met mine as the world bleached, and then blasted out color. I gritted my teeth with the ferocity of the climax. My body sizzled with my shudders, the culmination of hours of orgasms that overflowed into pure, untarnished pleasure. A tear dripped down my face as I melted, finally coming down off my high and relishing his weight pressing me down into the mattress.

He kissed me again, a sweet meeting of the lips that fluttered my heart. "Rest, baby. I'll be here all night." He moved until he was curled around me possessively, pulling me into his chest with his strong arms.

Chapter 9

F ILTERED SUNLIGHT SPRINKLED down onto the bed as I slowly came to consciousness. I rolled to my back and stretched, greeted by a glorious ache in a very private area. Hunter walked from the bathroom in gray slacks and an open button-up shirt. His hair was wet and a toothbrush hung from his mouth.

"Honeymoon's over, huh?" I asked with a laugh, propping myself onto an elbow.

"What?" he asked around the plastic.

"Nothing. Tired of jeans?"

He glanced down and then refocused on me. "You're beautiful, and yes. I can stop pretending to be young and hip."

"You are young and hip."

"Just young." He winked at me, easier and more relaxed than I'd ever seen him.

He leaned over his computer that stood open on the desk, reaching forward to type something before he closed the top and unplugged it. He scrubbed at his teeth a little more before disappearing into the bathroom. When he came out he said, "I want to put on my professional face today."

"So, what's the agenda?"

He packed his computer into its bag. "I have a meeting with Bruce to plan out some next steps, and then we'll be traveling back to San Francisco at about noon. You have the morning to pack."

I didn't mention that I'd never really unpacked.

"What about you?" I glanced at his suitcase in the corner and saw an empty suitcase stand. By the door his luggage waited, closed and ready to go. "Oh. You're ahead of me. What time did you get up?"

"I generally get up early," he said, running his fingers through his hair before smoothing it down with a brush and some product. He dropped those last items into the garbage. Apparently he'd rather buy new toiletries than pack them.

I pushed the blankets aside and threw my legs over the side of the bed, looking for my discarded T-shirt. I took the few steps to pick it up and throw my head into it. When I glanced over, Hunter stood transfixed, staring at me with lust-filled eyes.

"Like YMCA, do you?" I put my arms through the holes. "I have hundreds of dollars of lingerie, and you're crazy for my raggedy old shirt."

Hunter grinned as he sauntered toward me. "I've never seen a girl dressed down. Last night there was an honest quality to your messy hair, your shirt, and your sleepy smile that…made me want that."

When he reached me, his intense eyes delved into mine as his thumb traced my lips.

"Want what?" I asked in a whisper.

He kissed me lightly, his lips lingering. "Want a woman who doesn't try so hard. Who's comfortable in a big T-shirt and without makeup. Who will smile at me the moment she wakes up because she's happy to see me, instead of being happy to see my money or position. I want the normalcy you take for granted."

He ran his lips over mine again. Heat unfurled in me, a warmth that wasn't just sexual. One that was a lot more permanent. His hands felt up my stomach, under my shirt, before cupping my breasts. His kiss deepened as he pushed me backward. My back bumped the wall as his thumbs rubbed across my sensitive nipples.

"Hmmm," I moaned into his mouth.

Suddenly I needed him so bad I couldn't think straight. With shaking hands I fumbled with his pants, ripping open his fly and reaching inside to capture that velvety-smooth skin. I pushed his pants down as I ran my palm along his manhood.

His hand reached between my legs, fingers running along my slit. His other hand ran along the back of my leg to my knee before pulling upward. He hooked my thigh around his middle as he leaned in, his tip sliding along my wetness.

He lightly sucked my bottom lip as his erection probed me, sliding to my opening. With one shove, his girth filled me, a momentary burst of pain making me wince as he rubbed my soreness.

"Are you okay?" he asked against my lips.

I didn't bother answering. I threw my arms around his shoulders and swung my other leg upward. Clutching his middle with my thighs, I rocked into him. Soreness turned to exquisite pain, spreading in my body languidly. Gyrating my hips, I started a fast pace, which he met without hesitation.

His hard body pushed me into the harder wall. His length seared into me. His hips slammed against me as pain fell away, to reveal only unyielding pleasure.

I clutched his muscular shoulders as my body turned into liquid magma. I was close and we had only just started.

Luckily, so was he. "I need to come," he said in a moan as his body worked in deep, hard thrusts.

"Yes…" I matched his movement with rocking hips. Everything tightened. I held my breath in the moment before I exploded in a cry of delight. "Holy hell!" The *thunk* of my head hitting the wall competed with our mingled panting.

I let my limbs go limp.

Hunter grunted, having to shift so as not to drop me. I chuckled but didn't help.

He helped me straighten up and looked down into my eyes. "I want to take you home and make out."

I probably shouldn't have laughed, because he was absolutely serious, but…I couldn't help it. "Like high school."

"I didn't go to high school. I missed out on some things."

"Then making out sounds great." I ran my hands up his chest. "We could start now, even."

His smile stole my breath as he turned away. "Later. Business first. Play later."

By the time he'd crossed the room, the smile had already been wiped away. He picked up his computer and headed for the door. "Pack up. I'll meet you back here."

"Okay. I'll probably go work on Bruce's notes at the lagoon area, so if you get done early, that's where I'll be."

He gave a brief nod before leaving the room.

"Okay…*goodbye.*" I rolled my eyes. He might be a big-time CEO with oodles of money, but he was still a work in progress. I would definitely teach that kid manners.

Smiling like an idiot, I headed back to my room to get ready. What I was doing with Hunter might be incredibly stupid, but I didn't care. It felt good. *I* felt good. Repercussions be damned.

AT ABOUT TEN thirty I wandered into the lagoon area. I lowered myself onto a table and hauled out my computer. After signing in, I clicked out of instant message and didn't bother opening email. Hunter had given me a pass, and I planned to use it. I'd been thinking about Bruce's notes, and his goals, and had come up with a list of things that might be cool. I bent to my work and shut out the world.

It was because of the extreme focus, however, that I missed the person entering my oasis of solitude. I didn't notice the presence until the table shifted and creaked as someone sat opposite me. Forced out of my concentration, I glanced up in irritation. And then froze.

Rodge sat with his hands clasped in front of him, staring at me with hard, cunning eyes. "You've become quite a nuisance to me."

Feigning indifference, I glanced back at my computer screen. "I'm just doing my job."

"So it would seem." The top of my laptop slammed down. Rodge's fingers splayed across the top, white from the pressure. I looked up, startled. "My son gives a command, and you tear off your panties to please him. I should've expected a lowborn *peasant* to adopt tunnel vision for her rich boss. I underestimated your drive to please your betters."

"Peasant? Betters? Did you just fall out of 1890 and crack your head? Get off my laptop."

Rodge stood slowly, his hand still on my computer. He walked around the table with predatory steps before sitting right next to me. I scooted away to allow more room, but he just leaned in. His breath, smelling of stale coffee, blasted my face as he said, "I wonder. If I fucked you just right, would you do my bidding as well as you do his? What do you think, Olivia?"

Chest tight, breath coming in horrified puffs, I stood in a rush. "I need my computer, please." I snatched my computer bag off the table and held it in front of me. It was a terrible shield for a man of Rodge's size, but it was something.

He stood, too. His body cut off my view of my computer. "What's the matter? Afraid you'll like it too much?"

Rodge stepped toward me and grabbed a fistful of my hair. Before I could struggle, he yanked me closer. His lips smashed into mine.

My brain fumbled, deciding between stomping on his foot and kneeing him in the nuts. Without warning, his body was ripped away from mine. My head jerked before he let go. I staggered and fell, only then seeing another pair of feet.

I looked up. A sob of relief took me as Hunter stepped between his dad and me. His fist whipped out, clipping his dad on the chin and sending him to the ground.

"What the fuck are you doing?" Hunter demanded, his body flexed and fists balled.

Rodge turned onto his side and grabbed his jaw. He shook his head. "You always did like the ordinary ones, didn't you? Always trying to shrug off your wealth and status to go chasing the gutter rats. And now I know why. They work like slaves. Kudos, son. Looks like I'll have to get a gutter rat of my own."

"Always trying to be someone different than you," Hunter spat. He turned toward me and looked down for a moment before his mask of rage melted into guilt. He bent to me and picked me up out of the dirt. "Are you okay?"

"Yes." I wiped off my jeans as tears rolled down my face. I clutched Hunter, my hands shaking. "He scared me, is all. I just didn't react in time."

Hunter threw his dad a look of pure loathing before leading me to the table to help me collect my computer. With his hand around my shoulder, he turned us toward the path to the golf cart.

"Dating below your class is suicide," Rodge warned in a loud voice. "She'll drag you down and make a fool of you. I should know—I was with your mother for sixteen years. You'll see it my way before this is through. Trust me."

Hunter didn't say anything as he helped me into the vehicle and we drove back to our building in silence. It wasn't until we were headed to our rooms that he said, "I thought it was consensual at first." His voice was low, dripping with emotion. He leaned against the doorframe with a lowered head. "I walked into the area and all I saw was you kissing him. I…" His jaw clenched and he straightened up. He shook his head and looked away. "I'm sorry about that."

"Obviously I wouldn't," I said in a small voice.

Hunter turned toward his room. "Not with him, maybe, but you're free outside of your time with me." He shook his head again and let himself into his room without another word. I stood, lost for words, as the door shut behind him. The hard *clank* echoed down the hallway.

In a daze, unsure of what had just happened, I entered my room. The clock read nearly twelve. My suitcases were all packed and ready to go, and I stepped forward to go into Hunter's room and check in with the next steps. Before I got there, though, the door to Hunter's room swung closed. He'd locked himself away from me.

Not really believing it, I stared for a minute at that white surface. His words rang through my memory again. *You are free outside of your time with me.*

I sat on my bed, processing.

Apparently he thought I was the kind of girl he usually employed. I'd do him in the afternoon, and head home to someone else. Why stop at one guy—I could have a couple. Hell, I could have a whole swarm of guys ready to drop trow when I got horny. Three, four—why not a whole football team?

I stood in a rush of anger. A moment later, hardly in control, I banged on the connecting door with a closed fist. The whole floor probably heard it, but I didn't care. This was bullshit. I was tired of being dicked around by this guy.

The latch sounded before revealing his face, perfectly composed. His business mask was on; he was trying to close himself off from emotion.

I had enough emotion for the both of us.

"I'm sick of this, Hunter. I get that you have issues. I do. But guess what? We *all* have issues. We all have crap that went wrong. You can't use that as a reason to sling shit at everyone else. You're worried because you gave me *permission* to screw others. Well, guess what—screw *you*! I'm not that kind of girl. You know I'm not. So what you are doing here, this scared little boy routine, is bullshit. It's *bullshit*. And you're an asshole!"

I was blubbering by the end. His expression hadn't changed. He wore that same distant mask that he always did, trying to push me away. Again. Even after last night. After what he'd demanded I feel last night.

My heart felt like it was ripping in half. Angry tears rolled down my face.

I braced my hands on my hips. "That's it, then? You're freezing up on me?"

A knock sounded at his door. He glanced that way before looking back at me. I saw a glimmer of emotion in his eyes before his usual chill returned. "I'm sorry."

Pain and anger mixed together into one explosive cocktail. "I cannot believe this. One thing goes wrong, you get scared, and that's it? You are such a coward, Hunter. Plain and simple. Not noble, not smart, you're a coward that hides behind his big office and wads of cash. You might be fooling yourself, but you're not fooling me!" I turned away.

I ignored the agony eating away at my heart as I opened the door and carried my suitcase into the hall. I knew he felt something for me. After last night, there was no doubt. But if he wasn't willing to accept it, then I couldn't wait around like a fool. I had to learn my lesson sometime.

It was a quiet trip back to San Francisco. Silent tears leaked down my face, but I didn't apologize. I worked on Bruce's project and tried to shut off, like Hunter was doing.

It wasn't until the limo pulled up to my apartment building that Hunter spoke. "I don't blame you for my father," he said softly. He looked out of his window. "But I can't do this, Olivia. There's a reason I'm shut off. I don't do love. I can't do romance. Or forever. I just…can't. I'm sorry."

"We aren't doing romance. We are fucking, right? And I'm not asking for forever, Hunter."

"We aren't fucking, Olivia. Not anymore. Not after last night, and truthfully, not since the first time. It never would've been fucking with you." Hunter clasped his hands in his lap and looked down at the floor between his feet. "I can't repeat what we did last night. I can't give that much. I don't want to trust in that way."

"Can't. Won't. Don't want to." Another hot tear rolled down my face. "So many walls." I wiped my cheek. "Fine. No more sex."

"No." Hunter studied his hands. "No more, period. I crossed the line when I kissed you. I made you something else. And I can't be in that position. I can't stand the thought of someone else touching you. If you chose another…I wouldn't be rational. The situation is completely black and white for me. I cannot be with you and maintain my composure. In any capacity."

The pain in my heart bowed my whole body forward. Breathing became intense as I struggled not to sob with the tone in his voice. Because I knew that tone. I'd heard it before, most recently with Jonathan. It was the "I'm sorry" tone. The "let's be friends" tone. Except Hunter didn't want to be friends. He wanted to push me so far away he'd never think of me again.

Another hot tear made a trail down my cheek. "So…what happens now?"

"I'll place you in another position next week. I'll make up any difference in pay until you are elevated within your professional career to your current salary. I'll arrange for a safe to be put in your apartment for your jewelry. I think that's the only way."

Stunned, I stared at him. I didn't know what to say. I probably should've expected this, but since day one he always said he should give me up but wouldn't. I guess I'd believed him. And now I was floored.

"I'm sorry, Livy," he went on. "I can't have the distraction. This is how it has to be."

"Will you get another admin?" It was the first thing that came to my mind.

"Yes," he said in a flat voice.

"One like you usually get? With a contract…"

"Yes."

The pain twisted my gut. Sobs came up, choking me. "Is it because I'm lower on the social ladder than you?" My voice was small and wispy, but I had to know.

"Nothing my father said applies here, Olivia. He resented my mother because it was her money that dug him out of a failed business venture, but she was from the same social standing as he. Her father had humble beginnings, but by the time she was born, he was well into his millions. As for you, none of that matters. If that was the issue, I wouldn't need to make these changes. I have enough money for three lifetimes of indulgent living. The problem is that I can't have the attachment with you while still focusing on what's most important. We've crossed a threshold, which was my fault, and now there is no way back."

The tone and look of finality finally did me in. I'd hardly known Hunter Carlisle. It had been just a month. But I'd opened up in a way with him that I hadn't with anyone else. I'd let him in, feeling safe, and last night, feeling loved.

I'd meant to get out of the car before breaking down, but I didn't make it that far. I put my face in my hands and sobbed. I don't really remember getting into my apartment, just that Hunter picked me up and carried me into my room. He gave me one last kiss, deep and sensual, before turning around and walking out.

Chapter 10

I SHOWED UP to work on Monday with puffy eyes and a slump in my shoulders. I'd basically cried all weekend. I hadn't called anyone, I hadn't gone out, I'd barely eaten, and I'd been utterly miserable. I could call it the worst breakup I'd ever been through, but it wasn't even a breakup. I'd have to be *with* the guy for him to break up with me.

I dropped my laptop on my desk and looked up for Hunter's coffee as Brenda came down the hall with two cups in hand. She took one look at me and stopped dead. "What happened?"

"Guy trouble." I shrugged in that miserable way brokenhearted women did. I probably didn't even need to say anything, just give that shrug. Oh yeah, and look like absolute crap. Nailed on both counts.

"Ah. That's the worst kind of hurt." She put the coffee on the edge of my desk and surveyed me over her half-spectacles. "Breakup?"

"Something like that." I picked up Hunter's coffee.

"Did you kick the bastard in the balls? It doesn't solve anything, but it sure helps the mood."

I chuckled as my heart wrenched. "It would make me feel worse. Isn't that a bitch? He's being a scared little punk, but I can't hold him accountable, because he's doing what he promised he would do." I shook my head miserably. "I should kick myself."

"Why add injury to insult? Well, you just go in there and deliver that coffee. Interrupt his morning, if you want. He'll bark obscenities at you and send you running. It'll take your mind off things."

"Hunter swear at an employee?"

"He's in a foul mood today. Which doesn't make sense, as you landed the guy for him. Right?"

I moved toward the office, desperate to see Hunter's face, but dreading it all the same. "Stole him right out from under Hunter's slimy father."

"Good. That rat deserves it." Brenda moved around her desk as I entered the office.

The light shone in as it always did, cascading around Hunter's large shoulders and glancing off the side of his handsome face. I slowed, savoring the view. Remembering his kiss.

When I got to his desk, I put his coffee in the usual spot and noticed his shoulders tighten. He didn't turn to look, though.

With a stiff back and tears coming to my eyes, I turned quickly and walked out, then settled into my chair and stared at my desk for a moment. It was Brenda's glance that had me pulling out my laptop and firing it up, pulling up emails that I would never work on.

I pulled up instant message and fired off a question, not daring to go into Hunter's office to ask it personally.

Olivia Jonston: What should I work on?

Hunter Carlisle: Pull up the various job openings and see if anything fits your desires.

Nail. Hammer. Coffin. Today sucked.

I wiped a stray tear from my face and clicked into the intranet. I kind of wanted to pull a Milton from *Office Space* and set fire to the place. At the very least break a fax machine. Office violence seemed mandatory in this situation.

I saw Brenda look over again. I should probably stop sighing so loudly. Or did I sniffle?

"I'm not going to turn into a puddle of misery. I've been here before," I assured her. "This too shall pass, and all that."

"It's just…have you decided to leave?"

I couldn't stop my shoulders from hunching. "Ah. That. Is Hunter looking for a new admin already?"

"He's having me set up interviews. The first he scheduled himself for later today. He's in a hurry."

My gut twisted. It felt like a Buick was sitting on my chest. In as nonchalant a voice as I could manage, I said, "Yeah. Probably doesn't want to lose momentum with Bruce. The buyout, I mean."

I could see Brenda's stare for a moment longer out of

the corner of my eye before she said, "That's my girl. He didn't give you what you wanted, and you stuck it to him, huh? Well, good. He'll do this—he acts like a spoiled little baby when he doesn't get his own way, but he'll come around. Don't you worry. It'll eat away at him until he buckles. Just hold out."

I shook my head as a tear leaked out, thankfully on the opposite side of my face Brenda could see. I couldn't very well tell her this was all his doing, because that would raise questions. I didn't want questions. The situation was embarrassing enough.

Instead, I started looking through job listings, trying to find something out of the city, preferably, where I wouldn't even have to be reminded of him.

THE DAY PASSED in a slow grind of boredom. There were no questions to deal with, and I'd been through all the departments that were hiring. Most jobs sounded terrible, so I started looking at the departments that weren't hiring. Maybe Hunter would pull some strings.

The elevator chimed. Brenda murmured, "Brace yourself. Incoming."

I glanced up in a fog of misery to see a tall, beautiful blond saunter in wearing an expensive suit and displaying miles of cleavage. Brown eyes and a pretty face decked out in makeup smiled in a condescending way as she laid eyes on Brenda.

"Hello, I'm Candice, here to see Mr. Carlisle." She batted her eyelashes as Brenda checked her in before glancing at me. A tiny line developed between shapely eyebrows, probably at my appearance, before refocusing on Brenda.

"Please have a seat and he'll call you in," Brenda said, pointing toward the waiting area.

The woman turned gracefully on her high-dollar heels. My breathing got shallow and heavy as my heart started to ache, knowing that Hunter might just try her out today. Right now. He'd touch her intimately, only twenty feet away, while I sat, pining over him.

I bowed my head over my computer, seeing the keyboard turn foggy as my eyes filled with tears.

"He'll see you now," Brenda said.

The woman sauntered by, walking on those heels like she'd worn them all her life. Quite the contrast from my wobbling and staggering around.

"He won't go for her. Too tight-ass."

I ignored Brenda as I opened the programming notes from Bruce. I had nothing else to do, so I figured I might as well get lost in codes and programming. It was the only place I could totally shut off.

Half an hour later, the woman walked back out with stars in her eyes. She took a long look at me before thanking Brenda and strolling toward the elevator.

I hunched closer to my desk, trying harder to get lost in Bruce's new game. My heart hurt so bad that concentration was not just difficult, it was nonexistent.

THE NEXT DAY was the same, but thankfully, there were

no interviewees. Four were scheduled for the day after, though.

I spent the whole day working on Bruce's stuff, communicating with him freely via email, and sneaking out once for a phone call. That was when Kimberly caught me, having tried to get a hold of me since Sunday night.

"Livy? Is everything okay? I heard that Hunter Carlisle is looking for another admin."

"I don't really want to talk about it, but yeah. He is. I'll probably go somewhere else in the company."

"What happened?"

"Nothing. It's just better this way. Anyway, I have to go. I'll talk to you soon, okay?"

"Okay, but *call* me. I'm worried about you!"

"Okay, bye." I hung up and faced the breeze, willing the tears to stop running. Willing the hurt to subside so I could focus on something else besides this terrible ache in my chest.

WHEN WEDNESDAY ROLLED around, I was a nervous wreck. I knew the real applicants would come in, and I'd glanced at a few résumés. These women weren't just overqualified, they were spectacular. Experienced and already high-powered, these women were probably taking pay cuts to work for Hunter. He had the pick of the litter, and I was positive they'd all be beauties.

I slunk in, with my hair down and partially draped over my eyes. Brenda wandered to my desk, a little later than usual, set the cup of coffee down, and stood idle. I didn't bother looking up—I looked worse than I had for the last two days. I'd even had a stranger stop me on the way in and ask if I needed help.

When perfect strangers spoke up, things were not going well.

"You're in the home stretch, Olivia," Brenda said softly. "He can't hold out for much longer. He looks just as bad as you do."

I couldn't stop myself from glancing up then. Her expression was pure pity, her usually snarky visage softened with concern. It sounded strangely like she knew what was going on. What was *really* going on.

"What are you talking about?" I said. It was a bad cover, but I didn't know what else to say.

She tilted her head and gave a small pout before moving away to her desk. "I know what love looks like. And I know much more than you think. You've put that man on his toes. You've made him uncomfortable, you've made him bend, and now you're breaking him. His first reaction to things he can't control is to force them away. And now here you are, coming in every day when most women wouldn't, taunting him with your presence. And you look like hell, girl. He is a caring man underneath—he won't like to see his handiwork on the face of someone he cares about. Home stretch."

Tears leaked down my face as I cried softly toward my desk.

"You must think I'm daft not to know what a weird

setup he has with all these hoity-toity idiots. Useless, the lot of them." Brenda sniffed. "Finally he gets someone who won't fall into that ridiculousness, and he tries to chase her away? Well, I gave him a piece of my mind. Bert did, too." Brenda tsked. "I don't even care if he follows through and does fire me. Let's see him fill this spot, the spoiled little brat."

I took a deep breath and wiped my face, trying to tune out Brenda's muttering. It was naive to think she didn't know about Hunter's setup. I didn't even know if I had thought she had been oblivious to it. But discovering that she did know, and was on my side, made me feel better, if a little embarrassed. At least I wasn't alone.

I slouched the whole way into his office, staring at the ground. I put his coffee in the usual spot and turned. Before I'd made it to the door, though, he stopped me. "You don't need to come in for the rest of the week. I'll pay you for it, but it might be best if you stayed at home…"

Each word was a dagger into my heart. He'd probably be giving the second interviews, bringing in fresh girls, and sending them back out with a flush and a satisfied smile. Claws of pain raked down my middle as more tears dripped out. I nodded mutely, unable to utter a word.

Back at my desk, I opened my program again and just went to work, numbing my mind. Trying to block out the pain.

Ding.

I looked up with wary eyes as another blond bomb-shell walked into the room. Her hair was shorter and her eyes were hazel, but she could've been cut from the same cloth. The knockout cloth.

I looked back down at my computer, blocking out her sexy hum. I ignored her hippy saunter to the waiting area. And finally, I ignored the tear dripping down my face as she walked by my desk after being called into Hunter's office.

"When are the others coming?" I asked Brenda, not looking up.

"Why don't you take a long lunch?" Brenda said softly. "Come back at two. Everything should be over by then. He won't see these women for long."

I grabbed my handbag and walked out of the office, my mind on that beautiful, experienced, high-powered woman in there with Hunter, flirting and seducing him with her eyes. She probably hoped he would take her right there. And maybe he would.

I sat at a cafe with a coffee and an untouched sandwich for two and a half hours. Just sat there, staring at nothing. Images of Hunter kept flashing through my mind. Sweet things, like him holding the door open for me, or guiding me around, or our dance. Then the kissing. I felt the burn of his passion, so fresh in my memory. His shaking hands after we lay in a tangle of limbs. His soft words.

I sighed and shifted my unfocused gaze. Another tear dripped down my cheek.

I flinched as my phone vibrated on the table. I stared down in confusion, forgetting I'd brought it out at all. Hunter's name showed up above a text. "Come back to the office. Please."

I smiled a little at the *please* before throwing my coffee in the trash. The sandwich I gave to a homeless man asking for change outside. He glanced up with thanks, looking weary and downtrodden.

He looked exactly how I felt.

Back at the office, I passed by Brenda's empty desk and stopped at Hunter's door. I peeked through the vast and sunlit space, seeing him sitting at his desk, turned in his chair toward the window.

I walked in slowly, pain still eating away at my insides. "You wanted to see me?"

He turned around, showing that handsome face and those deep brown, turbulent eyes. "Yes. Have you found a new position?"

I took a seat in his visitor chair, not because I thought I'd stick around for long, but because I just didn't have any strength anymore. He'd defeated me. This whole situation had beaten me. I felt it in every nerve in my body.

"I found one that could work. It's in Windsor."

"Windsor?" Hunter's brow furrowed. "Way up north?"

"Yes. It's cheaper up there, and I could get a car. Seems like a good place. More bang for my buck."

Hunter braced his elbows on his desk. "It's a long

way. What about your family?"

"It's only an hour north with a car. And it's not much further from my mom than San Francisco is. Not that it would really matter She has her own thing going."

Hunter stared at me for a moment then bent down to the desk. "If that's what you want."

I clasped my hands in my lap. It wasn't. None of this was what I wanted. Getting away from him, though, would be the only way to heal. It would be the only way I could forget that a piece of him was still lodged deeply inside my heart from that intense, emotional night we'd spent together. From all our time together.

"Okay. I'll arrange everything. Brenda will contact you with the details." Hunter looked at his computer, but I could tell his eyes weren't reading what was on the screen.

"What about my computer? And should I give the credit card to you or Brenda?"

He shook his head in small jerks. "The computer will be needed in your next position. Keep that with you. And keep the credit card, in case you need something."

"I won't need anything, Hunter. You gave me a job. I'm all set."

His arms flexed. His gaze hit mine, powerful and intense. "Keep it. You'll need a new place to live, maybe new furniture—"

"I'll just leave it with Brenda." I stood and turned for the door.

"Olivia."

I paused, glancing back. Fire lit his eyes and his jaw clenched. He stared, not saying anything.

"Is that it for today?" I asked. "This is the exit interview, I take it…"

To his continued silence, I turned and walked from the room. I tidied up my desk, took the last of my personal items, left the credit card on Brenda's desk, and cried as I made my way home.

Chapter 11

I JUMPED WHEN my phone rang. I'd been sitting in my room, staring at the wall. Normal people would probably have been staring out the window, but really, what was the difference? I wasn't seeing anything anyway.

I held my phone up so I could see the screen, expecting it to be Kimberly. I'd filled her in on what had happened with Hunter shortly after my last day, needing to purge, and now she called daily, sometimes more, to check up on me. I got the impression she was worried that I would haul myself to the Golden Gate Bridge and do a swan dive off it.

A shock ran through me at seeing Bruce's name on my phone, having a hard time replacing the misery of love gone wrong. I knew he had my number, but he'd never called it before. He always emailed me with questions. For him to call me at all, let alone on a Saturday, was definitely odd. Or an emergency.

I swiped the phone before holding it to my ear. "Hello?"

"Livy, hi. It's Bruce."

"Oh hey—"

"Listen, I hear you're changing jobs. What's up?"

A laugh died in the back of my throat. The man was nothing if not bold and a little pushy. Pain rushed in to cover the delight, as I remembered how alike he and Hunter were when it came to focus and work ethic. They'd probably be an excellent team. Better than Hunter and I were.

Hand shaking, I swallowed down a sob. After a deep breath, I said, "I'm going to do something a little more up my alley, I think."

"He said you'd be in the IT department. That right?"

"Yeah. Yes. Yup." What was this, a lesson on how many ways to give an affirmation?

"That's not totally in your wheelhouse. Sure you'd be any happier there than as an admin?"

"I—"

"Because listen, I've been thinking. We're on to something. I really think we've created some magic. If we pull this app off how I think we will, it's going to lead to dollars. If we put that money back into our product, like Hunter suggested, and use that momentum, I'd bet we have the makings of a great business here, Livy."

I resumed my stare at the wall. I didn't want to think of business, because that made me think about Hunter. And *that* lead to thoughts on who he got to replace me. He might've had someone right at that moment, bent over his desk, giving herself to his pleasure. She'd have a contract, and new clothes, and Hunter's time.

I heaved a sigh as tears filled my eyes. "I thought you wanted to get out of business."

"I'll need *something* to do. My wife can't possibly want me hanging around the whole time. If we just keep it small, I think it would be a fine day job."

"That's probably what you said about the last startup. And look how that turned out…"

I heard a bark of laughter. "Yes, but I know what I'm doing this time. Mostly. Still, I'll have you. You're a rock of sense."

I huffed.

"I really think we can do this, Olivia."

I wiped a tear off my cheek. "I'm just the helper. I don't know much about business."

The line was silent for a moment. When Bruce spoke again, his tone was softened. "Look, Livy…I don't know what went wrong, but I do know that removing yourself totally from the situation might be best. I'll beat whatever Hunter is paying you. I have faith that we'll make money once this gets going. You'd be great on my team. We work well together, our ideas are tight, and our programming is top-notch. Together we can make magic. I really believe that."

I shook my head miserably, but I couldn't help believing in his conviction. Not only that, but his words rang true. We *were* a great team. We *did* create some great stuff when we put our heads together. And I'd finally be able to do what I loved. Just not with the man I was growing to love.

"I don't know, Bruce. I need some time to think about it." I leaned back against my headboard. "For now, I'll still work on the notes and help out. I just don't know that I'm ready to be a partner."

"I'm having a contract drawn up—you already *are* a partner, Livy. You need to get paid for what you're helping with. I'll have my secretary send it over. This would just be formalized."

I groaned. "Not more contracts!"

"Listen, I have to go. I'm supposed to be in a meeting. But think about it, okay? You love this work—don't try to tell me you don't. And with the buyout, your salary will be secure. There's no reason to say no."

"I'll think about it."

"Think hard. Okay, see ya."

The line went dead. I pulled the phone away from my head, making sure the call had ended, before dropping my hand to the bed.

There was a reason to say no. I'd be officially separating myself from Hunter. Right now I was moving away, yes, but I would still be in the same company. I'd still get emails from the CEO's office. I could still easily chat with Brenda in a work capacity. And yes, I would still have the opportunity to see Hunter, however remote. In his company, I was still within his circle of influence, no matter how removed. If I left, I'd be tearing myself away for real. For good. That would be the end.

I shuddered in a sob. It felt like my heart was clawing out through my chest.

I should leave Hunter's company. I should leave Hunter.

My phone rang again. This time it was Kimberly. I silenced it and heaved myself off the bed. In a fog, I left my phone behind and made my way out of my apartment and down to the street. I walked to the bus stop and boarded the next bus, out of spite.

I couldn't deny that I wanted to work for Bruce. His project was as fun as it was rewarding. Writing the code, and then watching what it created, sparked my happy sensors. I felt at home with it in a way that I never felt I belonged in the admin role.

I belonged in that job the same way I belonged with Hunter.

I wiped another tear from my face as I stared out of the bus window. The woman next to me hawked a loogie and spat it into a paper bag. That action wasn't as revolting to me as leaving Hunter for good.

"I'm in a fix," I muttered at the window.

I was surrounded by people, but none of them even turned my way. They ignored me chatting to myself, just like they ignored the woman spitting into a bag. Welcome to public transportation in San Francisco.

If I took Bruce's job, I could stay in the city. Near Hunter.

I ran my hand over my eyes. "I'm just not getting the picture. He doesn't want me!" I mumbled furiously.

In a way, it kind of felt good to blend in with the

crazy people that frequented the bus system. I felt crazy. I felt like I was losing a piece of myself. A very important, central piece.

I thought of my dad. I wanted to tell him my woes, cry in his arms, and listen to his words of wisdom. He'd know what to do. He'd know how to help me.

As the bus made its slow way through the city, I knew where I needed to go to make a decision.

Chapter 12

"WHAT ARE YOU doing here?"

I stared at my mother with barely contained irritation. "I'm visiting the house I grew up in. I still have stuff here, or did you sell it all for more space?"

I pushed past her into the moderate space of her three-bedroom house located in San Rafael, a city north of San Francisco.

"At least you're not embarrassing," my mom said with a flat tone as she looked me over. I had on jeans, as normal, but I'd paired it with a nice sweater Hunter had bought me. I'd also done my hair and makeup, as Kimberly had instructed. She'd said the worst thing for a person with heartache was to mope. If I did myself up, looking good on the outside would make me feel better on the inside.

Turned out, she'd been completely wrong. But looking better on the outside made people *think* I was doing okay, and left me alone. That was enough.

"It's Sunday—aren't you supposed to be at a garden

party or something?" Only then did the murmur of voices drift to me from the living room.

"I'm having a small soiree here. I thought it might be nice for Sean to stay here while he's in town. More homey than a stuffy hotel in the city." My mom lifted her chiseled nose in the air. She'd had two nose jobs, both gifts from two different boyfriends.

"Sean is…new?" I asked.

"Yes." My mother smiled with plump lips she was not born with. "I met him at a party the other night. He's an investment banker."

"Huh. And how does his wife feel about you?"

She rolled her eyes. "He plans to get a divorce, so it doesn't really matter. All I have to do is hold on for a few months, and then snatch him up. After that, it's off to New York for me. He's just out here on business."

"Oh, right." I shook my head. The story was always the same, and my mother always believed them.

She surveyed my outfit again.

"Don't worry, I won't be in your way. I just want to get a few things and then I'll be gone."

My mother made a noncommittal sound and swished her blond hair away from her eyes. Without another word, she sauntered off toward the living room.

The woman was a knockout, even in her fifties. It was too bad she always went for wealthy men with wives and kids. She kept believing they'd leave their old lives and start over with her, but she always got turned down. If she kept on, she'd end up lonely and alone.

Not that I was doing any better. What did they say about a living in glasshouse with a pocketful of stones?

I slunk into my room and swiped my old teddy bear off my bed. The one thing my mom had done for me was keep my room as it was. I wasn't welcomed around all that often, as I cramped her style, but she did leave me just the tiny bit of my past that I clung on to with both hands in times like these.

I hugged my bear to my chest and dug my face into his soft, old head. Fresh tears fell, wetting his matted fur.

I longed for the past, when I would wait with this bear until my dad showed up for our weekend together. He loved me more than the breath in his lungs. We'd have such fun together, picnicking or watching a movie. Whenever I was heartbroken, or simply had a bad day, he'd just sit and listen to the sad tale, then hug me close, promising that someday I'd meet someone who would treat me like the treasure I was. Little did I know at the time that he was that man. He was the epitome of unconditional love, and now that he was gone, I felt like I didn't matter to anyone at all.

I heaved myself off my childhood bed and wandered into my mother's room. I exited to the backyard through her sliding glass door and found the old tire swing hanging from the oak tree in the corner of the brown square that used to be lawn. I settled myself onto it gingerly, monitoring the bend of the branch overhead. Satisfied that it would hold, I gently swung with my bear in my arms and let the tears come freely.

The sliding glass door rolled at the other side of the yard. Laughter rumbled through until my mother's high-pitched, excited chatter floated nearer. "See, there she is. She must've snuck out here, the little minx!"

I gave one of those shudder sighs that said my body hadn't recovered from the constant crying, and wiped my eyes on my sleeve. There was no telling who she was sending out to find me. Probably the cousin, nephew, or junior associate of the man she was dating. If she got me hitched with money, or even the prospect of money, she'd assume all her troubles would be over.

I rested my chin on the tire swing, waiting for the bachelor of the moment to saunter in front of me, thinking I was as easy as my mom.

"There now. Can I get you something? Are you sure you don't want some wine? Or sparkling water?" my mother asked, a few paces behind me.

"No."

Cold washed down my spine as I snapped my head around.

Hunter stood next to my mother in one of his tailored suits. Straight and tall, handsome and broad, he looked like a million dollars while standing in the wilderness of my childhood backyard. He slid his hands in his pockets as my mom winked at me and walked back. A few people looked out the sliding glass door at Hunter before my mother shooed them back into the house and closed the door.

Hunter's deep brown eyes, always hooded as though

just emerging from the throes of climax, gazed at me with regret and uncertainty. "Need a push?"

Aware that my face was probably still stained with tears, and worried it was streaked with worse, I turned away to wipe my eyes and nose on my sleeve. "No," I said with a hoarse voice. "I don't trust the branch to hold up."

I heard his six-hundred-dollar shoes crunch on the brittle, dead grass. He stopped in front of me, looking down on my face.

"What are you doing here?" I asked softly, not daring to meet his eyes. I knew better than to ask how he found me—the man could get whatever information he wanted, one way or another.

"Brenda doesn't put my coffee in the exact same place on the desk every time she brings it to me. She also doesn't smell like lilac on a fresh spring morning. She doesn't have the low, sultry hum to her voice, or the uncommon beauty I look forward to. Her hips don't sway in a completely unassuming way that still manages to catch every male eye in the vicinity. I don't want to look up from my work when Brenda walks away, as I always do with you. I don't want to touch her, or kiss her, or watch an embarrassed flush creep up her face. And I certainly don't want to do that with some other random admin after my cock or my money."

I blinked up at him, barely daring to believe what I was hearing.

"I missed you as soon as you walked out of my office," he continued. "I've not got anything done since you left. I might as well have stayed home. But home wouldn't have you there. And with you is where I want to be."

"But...your contract..." New tears were flowing now. Tears of hope. I was desperate to believe him.

He stepped closer and brushed his fingertips along my chin to lift my face. "I can't have you near, because you distract me, but banning you from my life completely derails me. A contract can't fix what's wrong with me. It was to prevent the feelings you are forcing me to feel. I can't go back to the way things were. I can't pretend I don't have feelings for you, Livy. So I find myself in uncharted waters."

"What does that mean for us? For you?"

He bent to brush his lips along mine. "I'd tell you to run, but I would chase you. I am chasing you. Come back to work for me."

I nodded, not trusting my voice.

His eyes softened as his lips turned up into a grin. "Good. I hoped I wouldn't have to beg."

"I didn't know begging was something you did."

"It isn't. Neither is breaking my own rules and getting attached. Or kissing. Yet with you, all I seem to do are things I usually don't." He bent and gave me a slow kiss. "Show me your bedroom. This is where you were raised?"

"You're not going to do a personality flip again, are you?" I asked, gingerly getting out of the tire swing.

With my luck, the branch holding it would break in half and crack me on the head.

"I hope not, because then I'd have another miserable week. I don't think I could go through that again." His strong arm wrapped around my waist, pulling me closer. "I'm sorry. For everything. You are a saint for sticking with me."

"I didn't really have much choice. Last week wasn't much better for me."

"I know," he whispered, touching his lips to mine again. He opened my mouth with his, flicking his tongue inside.

I fell headfirst into the kiss. My surroundings dropped away as I focused completely on his touch.

"Show me your room," he murmured against my lips.

I led him through the sliding glass door and my mother's bedroom until I could shut the door to my room with him inside it. Unable to wait, I pushed him against the door and captured his kiss again, sinking into the feeling of his lips moving against mine. I unbuttoned his shirt before sliding my palms along his smooth, muscled skin.

"Here?" he asked in a heavy voice. "Are you sure?"

"Yes." I pushed off his jacket before undoing his pants.

His hands slid up my sweater and covered my breasts. "Your mom won't come in?"

"That's what locks are for." I giggled, turning the

catch on the handle.

"I feel scandalous." He pushed down my pants before sucking in a breath as I took his hard length in my hand.

"Says the man who orders his admin to bend over the desk."

"Hmm." He walked me backward. "We'll do that tomorrow."

I turned us and pushed. He fell back onto my bed. I knelt over him and took his erection into my mouth. I tickled the tip with my tongue before sucking it in. He groaned.

I backed off, trailing my lips against his shaft, before sucking again. I took him deep into my throat, loving his hasty release of breath. I worked my hand in tandem with my mouth, seeing his muscles start to flex. I stopped and climbed on top of his body. I braced over him as his head came up and his hands grabbed my hips. I sat down.

A spark of color made me pause. "Oh, holy— Hmm." I smiled with my eyes closed, just feeling his size fill me up. I moved my hips in a circle. My smile melted as the sparks turned into bursts, lighting up my body.

His palms slid up my chest and cupped my breasts. His thumbs rubbed my nipples.

I blew out a breath as my sensual beginning turned into a harried gyration. I rocked forward and back, my hands braced on his chest and my head back. "Oh, Hunter," I said, bucking now. Working him inside of me. Feeling the friction.

His fingers clutched my hips. He lifted and then pulled back down. My body crashed onto his.

"Oh *shhhhhii*—" I rocked forward again, then back, before he picked me up and pulled. The tightness in my body started to pool in my core. Heat blazed, white hot. I rocked, then sat as he thrust up into me. My breathing turned ragged. Our movements were sloppy and fast, but perfect. Wild.

"Harder," I begged, face pointed upward. Muscles flexed. Fingers dug into him. "*Harder!*"

Hunter sat up and encircled me in his strength. He trapped me to his chest and bucked up into me. His size pierced me, forcing the breath from my lungs. My bed screamed against the floor. The end slammed into the wall.

"Oh… Oh!" I held on. Almost there. Another thrust. One more.

"Ahhh!" Fire spilled over and coursed through my body. I let out a glorious moan as an orgasm lit me up. I shuddered over Hunter as I felt him shake beneath me.

I grabbed his face and gave him a deep kiss, sucking in his tongue as I trembled on top of him. His hands slid up my back languidly. He lay down, controlled the whole way to the bed. His abs held both our weight. I had no idea why that impressed me as much as it did.

I snuggled my face up to his neck and just breathed in his familiar smell. Lord how I'd missed it.

After a while, he said, "I fell in love for the first time when I was barely sixteen. It was to one of our maids, a girl three years or so older. She was a beauty, with heart-shaped lips that always seemed to be pouting. I lusted after her immediately, of course—I was basically a constant hard-on at that age. I would've been entranced with any pretty girl, but as I was homeschooled, she was the only one I was around for any length of time."

Hunter's hand reached out slowly and traveled down my arm until he clasped my hand. "I barely flirted before she noticed me, and a short time later I was sneaking her into my room. I basically fell into intimacy. She wasn't a virgin, nor was she interested in taking it slow. Our first time making out, I felt all the intimate places on her body. The second, we both stripped down to our skin. The third I lost my virginity. Just like that. I loved it, though—as you would expect from a sixteen-year-old. I didn't have a clue about what I was doing, but she was always willing.

"After a while I wanted to spend more time kissing. Or just being together. She never did. Thinking back now, I realize I missed out on a lot of sexual enlightenment. Don't get me wrong, she taught me the ropes on how to please her, but when it came to me, she just lined me up and let me hump away like a rabid animal until it was over. Sex couldn't have been that much fun for her, but that realization came later. Too late.

"We kept on for a few months before my mother figured out what was going on. She sat me down one day and said that it wasn't exactly prudent for me to be fornicating—that's the word she used—with the hired help, but I would do as I pleased. She asked me, simply, that I use protection. Not only for safety, but because I was much too young to be having a child. I told her that Denise—that was her name—was on the pill. My mom never spoke against that, but she still asked me in her levelheaded way to take charge of my own fate. Use protection.

"My mother is a sensible, reasonable woman. She was always fair with me, even when I was being Satan's helper. I did as she asked. And oh, the fights that caused with Denise. She raged at me, and fought with me, and denied me, saying I didn't trust her. This just made me dig in my heels all the more. I don't respond well to that behavior. I'm too stubborn. Besides, my mother was right—I needed to take charge of my own fate. Denise started seducing me all over the house, often away from my bedroom—I suspect she was trying to get me away from my stash of condoms. I always had one on me, though.

"After a while, she stopped trying to get me to go unprotected, and instead, didn't want me as much. By this point, she was my world. Maybe it was all the drama that blinded me, that made everything so much more exciting, but I saw stars when I looked at her. I was completely in her power, and, I thought, thoroughly in love."

Hunter took a deep breath. His hand was shaking in mine. "And then one day she sat me down and told me that she was pregnant. We'd been intimate for about a year. I was seventeen. I asked how, and she said one of the condoms must have leaked."

Hunter's voice dripped with emotion now. He hugged me tight. "I was terrified at first, not to mention worried about what my mom would say, but I was determined to do the right thing. I offered to marry her, and she accepted."

He paused for a moment. I just waited quietly. Finally he went on. "After it all sank in…I was ecstatic. I'd never been happier. Something struck a chord in me as far as her pregnancy was concerned. I can't explain it. I just remember feeling so euphoric. I'd created life, and she was growing it inside of her. I was blown away."

He squeezed my hand. "But it didn't last. My mother and father were having screaming matches by that point. They hated each other, and finally, she kicked him out. That's when the whole, ugly truth came out. I got to Denise first, but he had more money. Even though he knew I was sexually active with her, he seduced her. Or maybe he just let her seduce him, I don't know."

Hunter's voice dripped with scorn. "I thought it was my baby, and that I was going to marry her. I'd bought her a ring, fantasized about a family and being a good father… Nope. He'd bought her a bigger ring, and then flaunted her in front of my mother—while indirectly flaunting her in front of me. It was then, as Denise was telling me that I had always been plan B, and terrible in bed, that she also revealed it wasn't my baby at all. It was my father's. He'd taken not only my first love, but what I thought was my baby and my future. He'd taken everything happy in my life for his own, and sneered that we could still share her if I wanted."

Hunter wiped moisture from his cheek. His voice shook with suppressed emotion. "I was a stupid kid. I'd had no experiences in life until that point. Sure, an adult would've seen her actions for what they were, but I wasn't an adult. My father *knew* I loved her. He *knew* I thought that baby was mine, and that I'd proposed. He knew, and he didn't give a shit. He let me go on thinking it until what he needed conflicted, and then took it."

"What happened to the baby?" I asked in a soft voice, holding his shaking hand in both of mine.

"She miscarried at six months. They couldn't save it."

"And your father—how did he take it?"

Hunter scoffed. "He never loved her. She was young and pretty, so he dressed her up and wore her to business functions like a coat. Outside of the public eye, however, he didn't concern himself with her or the baby. He had another mistress soon after they were married. She was a prop."

"Did you ever talk to her again?"

"A few times, just to check in. I offered to take her away from her soulless life with my father, but he had all the money, and I had an allowance. She wanted to stay with the money."

"Unhappy but rich."

"Exactly."

"And now?" I asked in a gentle voice.

"She got a settlement from my dad and married again—a younger man with some small wealth. She didn't try for any more kids—or if she did, she didn't carry to term."

"And so, you haven't kissed a woman since her?"

Hunter traced a line down my back. "I wanted to forget and move on. I've always been haunted by that experience. I was so, *so* happy, Olivia. When I saw her start to show, and kissed her stomach—with other women, that's all I could think about." His voice dropped again. "Until you."

Shivers racked my body as he hugged me again, resting his cheek on the top of my head.

"You're the first woman I've trusted without protection," he said quietly. "Don't bother asking me why—I don't know. Maybe I'm tired of controlling my own destiny. Maybe I want fate to step in and show me the way. But it feels right, and I trust you."

"No offense, but if the roles were reversed, no way would I trust you." I kissed his neck to make light of the comment. "Men are forgetful, and I can barely take care of myself."

He chuckled softly. "You don't need to take care of yourself. That's what I'm for." He kissed me on the temple. "Will you stay the night with me tonight? I don't know what comes next—we're back in the gray area. Life is chaos with you. But I would like to sleep near you."

"I could do with a little making out. And I'll say no a

few times, just to give you the sense of your first time…"

"You wouldn't be able to say no to me." I heard the passion ring through his voice.

"Challenge accepted."

Chapter 13

I STOOD FROM the bed and put my bear near my pillows. Hunter grabbed it as he stood. "To give you a little piece of home at my house."

I slipped my hand through his as we left the bedroom. We didn't make it far, though, without my mother sounding the alarm.

"Oh, honey, are you leaving so soon?" She rushed toward us with two glasses of wine. "Here, have a drink. Mingle!"

"We were just leaving, Mom." I pulled Hunter to the door.

"Nonsense—there are a few people who want to meet you and your illustrious guest. It's not often we have one of the business elite in this house. Now the house is full of them!" My mom playfully put her hand on Hunter's arm as she giggled.

A fifty-year-old giggling like a schoolgirl was a little off-putting, to say the least. Being that it was my mom as well—I wasn't really in the mood. Still, I rarely said no when she gave me an entreaty like this. Too much like my dad, I guess.

I glanced at Hunter. "A minute?"

He didn't respond, which meant yes. To my mother's delight, I led him through the foyer and to the living room beyond where a crowd of fifteen or so people stood around idly, chatting and sipping beverages. They all looked up as Hunter came in the room. A few eyes brightened. One man even stepped forward with an outstretched hand.

"Hunter Carlisle, what an honor!" The graying man shook Hunter's hand with vigor. "It's not often I see you outside of a business meeting."

"Mr. Evens." Hunter shook his hand before wrapping his arm around my middle.

"He came to see my daughter. This is—"

A tall man with silver hair stepped forward with an outstretched hand. "Mr. Carlisle, we've not met. I'm Sean Hutch. I've worked with your dad on a few projects."

My mother gave Sean a proud smile and laid her hand on his arm. "He's very successful."

Hunter took the hand with no expression before looking away. The smile wilted from Sean's face as he said, "I'm just out here for a quick business trip."

Hunter glanced at my mom before looking around the room in disinterest. "I'm sure your family misses you, but these things have to be done."

"You're not drinking your wine," my mom hastened

to say, reaching for Hunter's glass. "Can I get you something else?"

Hunter let her take the glass before turning more solidly into me. "I'm just waiting to escort Olivia home."

"We're ready." I put my untried glass on the coffee table behind me. "Let's go."

"So soon?" My mother followed us from the room like an earnest puppy. "Stay, you two!"

"I'll talk to you later, Mom." I pulled open the front door and stepped outside, greeted by the soft California sun in late fall. The chill had me crossing my arms, but not making me wish I'd brought a jacket.

"Well, okay. I'll call you soon!" My mom watched as Hunter led me to the street to a sleek gray sports car.

"Is that an Aston Martin?" I asked as we neared.

"Yes. I trust you didn't drive?"

"No. Bus." He opened the door for me and handed me inside. I sank down into the glorious leather as he slid into his side. The car roared to a start, high octane and full of power.

"Money isn't everything, but it sure can provide you with a nice ride." I marveled as he smoothly pulled away from the curb.

Hunter made his way through the tangle of streets. I thought back to my mom's quick change in demeanor. "She's never been that earnest with me. It was…weird."

"You two don't have a great relationship."

I snorted. "That's putting it mildly. I was a mistake that held her back. She thinks she would've landed a great catch had it not been for me."

"Yet she chose to let you live with her instead of your dad."

"There is that. She had a nicer house than my dad. Larger and better for a kid. That was part of the problem—she had to look after me. She couldn't just leave at a moment's notice. Her single life, and single body, was ripped away. But...you're right. She *did* sacrifice. She made the effort to be a mom. And maybe that's why I still keep in contact. And why I'll still help her if ever I can. She's not the best, but she's my mom. You can't turn your back on family."

It dawned on me who I was talking to. "I mean...you know, family that isn't trying to ruin me. Unlike your dad. I fully support turning your back on your dad. He's..." I picked at my nail. I couldn't get my foot further in my mouth if I tried. "I think I'll stop talking now..."

Hunter reached across the space. His fingers threaded through mine. "I like that you keep in contact with your mother. I think you two would find things easier if she had more security. It seems to me that she's in survival mode. You don't see clearly when you're worried for your future."

"Did you know my mom's new boyfriend?" I asked as he was making his way to the freeway. "Sean, I guess."

"Heard of him. He's a few years away from getting fired, or from landing in jail. His dealings are less than reputable."

"Yeah. I figured. My mom's getting desperate, I think. She's still stupidly pretty, but she's getting up there. Plastic surgery can only go so far." I looked out the window. "I wish I got some of her looks."

"You have her facial structure, but you have a natural beauty, whereas she is more manufactured."

I glanced at Hunter as the car lurched forward. The engine whined and picked up speed as we merged onto the freeway. From slow and steady to zooming past all the other cars in the space of a few seconds, we blasted into the fast lane before he let off the gas.

"She's had a lot of work done. She used to be a natural beauty," I said as I unpeeled my fingers from around the handle in the door.

"No. There are two types of beauty. One is the type that lends to hair dyes and plastic surgery. Those women can dress themselves up into what I call manufactured beauty, but they were really just pretty before that. Then there is your beauty. It's unique. It can't be bought. You assume that because society says you should have blond hair and huge eyelashes, and you don't, that you aren't gorgeous. When really, you're unspoiled, untarnished gold. You don't need makeup or hair dye. You look your absolute best with a big T-shirt and a sleepy smile."

I blinked back tears as I watched his face, utterly serious. "You do might not say please, but you do say the sweetest things."

"It amazes me that any of that is news to you."

"My father said something similar, but he doesn't

count." I wiped a tear from my cheek. "I've been living in my mother's shadow for a long time. She hated that I wasn't a mini-me."

"I know the feeling. You've met my father, after all."

"How about your mother? Did she ever remarry?"

Hunter's jaw tightened as anger flashed in his eyes. "No. She lost a lot of money in the divorce with my father—she'd brought the money to the marriage, but the prenup expired after ten years—my dad doesn't fight fair."

"Even with his mistresses?"

"California is a no-fault state. He was entitled to half, but he ended up with more since he sank a bunch into his company. She wasn't destitute, by any means, but the whole situation…turned her off marriage. She rarely dates. My father ruined her chance of happiness in many ways."

"That sucks."

"Yes."

We crossed the Golden Gate Bridge. The ocean sparkled below us, twinkling in the evening sunshine.

"My father died right before I went to college," I said as I looked out the window. "I miss him every day. He was such a good man. I spent my freshman year crying half the time. I think Kimberly was the only reason I made it through."

"She's a sweetheart, Kimberly."

"Yes. And she interviewed for you."

I just barely caught Hunter's quick glance. "Yes. Being my admin was no place for her. She would've become attached if she didn't start to hate me first. If she did get attached, and I had to let her go, she still would've ended up hating me. Not a good fit."

"But she's tougher about that stuff than I am."

Hunter turned off the main road. "I've already told you—I had to have you. There was no rhyme or reason for it; I just needed you. I knew you were the type to fall, and I knew you wouldn't be okay with my setup, but…I wanted you. I'm selfish."

"You're not selfish," I muttered. We wound back through the large houses toward the cliff overlooking the ocean. "You live in here?"

"My city house is here, yes."

"Didn't Robin Williams live back in here?" I watched the huge houses roll buy, larger and larger as we got closer to the ocean. "Wait, your *city* house?"

"I keep a residence here because it's closer to work, but I also have an estate in Napa Valley, as well as a of couple properties abroad."

"Of course you do," I said under my breath as we pulled into the garage of a mansion with a crystal-clear view of the limitless horizon beyond.

We got out of the car as the garage door closed. Shelves lined the sides of the space with labeled boxes and containers. It was the most organized garage I'd ever seen. Not a single thing looked out of place. While there was a toolbox, there were no stray tools littering any work tables.

"This is…not normal." I walked around to the other side of the car, toward the door leading into the house, trying to find something out of place. "Does anyone use the garage, because…this is weird."

He didn't answer. Apparently he didn't see my point of view.

With his hand on the small of my back, we walked through a door into a parlor decked out in earth colors, fine furniture, and oil paintings. He directed me through a hallway and into a living room with perfectly staged chairs, couches, and tables. A large entertainment center stood in the corner, and I noticed wireless surround sound speakers strategically placed around the room.

"Big." I didn't really know what else to say.

His grin had me blinking up at him as he led me from the room. "I'm never usually home this early— would you like to take a dip in the pool, or watch TV, or…"

"You're about to ask what normal people do with their free time, aren't you?" I asked with a laugh, leaning into his warmth.

"I can order food, if you want. What would you like for dinner?"

"Oh." I bit my lip. "I don't know—what delivers out here?"

His brow furrowed as he looked down at me. "Did you want takeout?"

"Maybe I'm hearing things. Didn't you just ask if you should order dinner…?"

Hunter led me through the room to a hallway on the other side. I tried to glimpse the art as we passed, only to suddenly stop in a large kitchen where a portly woman in a white apron was writing something as she leaned over the central island. She glanced up at our entrance. Her eyes widened. "Oh, Mr. Carlisle—you're home early. Is everything okay?"

"Good evening, Mrs. Foster. Yes, everything is fine. What did you have planned for tonight?"

"Well, Miss Englewood is having company tonight, so she's ordered appetizers. For you, I'd planned a pot roast."

My focus stuttered. It sounded like Blaire lived with Hunter, though I could've sworn that I'd always heard she led an entirely separate life…

Hunter looked down at me. "Do you like roast?"

"Homemade food I don't have to make? Yes! Roast, sandwiches—whatever. I'm in."

"Miss Jonston and I will take our meal in the dining room—or do you know where Blaire has planned her get-together?" He sounded like he was talking about a roommate. Which implied she did, in fact, live with him.

Mrs. Foster's smile at my roast and sandwiches comment dwindled. A disapproving look came into her eyes. "She'll probably be in the dining room at some point. I believe she has planned…" The older woman pursed her lips. "A sex party. It will be her, another gal, and a host of men, I believe."

My mouth dropped open in disbelief. I thought I

had roommate troubles...

Hunter's jaw clenched and his arm tightened around my waist. "I see. We'll stay in my room, then."

He steered me from the kitchen and we returned the way we had come until we were at the front of the house. A wide staircase led up to the second floor.

"So...Blaire lives here, huh?" I asked in a small voice.

"Part of the contract. She moved in the day after I signed. I rarely see her."

I nodded as though it was perfectly normal to treat one's fiancée with no more regard than a roommate, and then bring girls home when said fiancée was in the same house. I then put her from my mind. He was just newly resigning himself to wanting me back in his life. I didn't want to rock the boat so soon. If they rarely saw each other, she wouldn't be a problem for me.

We walked to the back of the house. Hunter let me into a massive room with a fireplace, a bathroom in the far corner, and a glass door leading out to a deck. Another large TV hung on the wall opposite the king-sized bed.

"Sure you have enough space?" I asked, glancing over the immaculate room.

"I spend most of my time here when I'm not working. All I really need is a bed."

"Uh huh." I looked at the four-poster monstrosity that would never fit in my own room.

"Would you like something to drink?" He crossed to a globe in the corner and pulled back the dome. Like in the movies, various kinds of alcohol waited in their crystal decanters. Luckily, beside the brown liquids he obviously drank, based on the levels in the containers, he also had an unopened bottle of wine. "I can have something brought up, too, if this won't work? A beer, maybe…"

"Nope, wine is fine." I sat on the edge of the bed, taking it all in. I was in Hunter Carlisle's house! I'd gone from reluctant admin, to sex buddy, to intimate partner, to on the outs, to seriously *in,* all in a little over a month. It had been a wild ride so far.

"So…Blaire's into orgies, huh?" I wiggled out of my shoes.

"Yes. Among other things. She speaks about class and status while performing some…interesting sexual acts." Hunter handed me the glass of wine before sitting next to me on the bed and looking at the blank TV.

"And you are…planning to marry her?" I said hesitantly.

"At first I was, but…" He took a sip of his drink. "Even without…changing circumstances, I have a hard time associating myself with someone who invades my home with strange fetishes. Having an orgy is one of her tamer occupations. Imagine if a business associate found out."

"So why is she still around? You know, if you aren't happy…" I was trying to be really blasé about this whole thing, but the thought of him marrying someone else, even if it didn't mean anything, was squeezing my heart in uncomfortable ways.

"We entered into a contract. It might be easier to marry her and then get the wedding annulled than call it off. I need to have my lawyer look at it."

"You and your contracts." I took a sip of my wine as my mind played over the "changing circumstances" comment.

"Yes." His eyes dipped to my lips. "Did you want to take a dip in the hot tub before dinner?"

"Normally I'd just say yes, but you have people in this house, and I don't have a suit. Or a solid-colored bra and panties."

Hunter stood and put his drink down on a dresser. He walked toward the bathroom, disappearing around the corner, before coming back with two robes. He laid them on the bed. "No one will bother us."

A flurry of butterflies assaulted my stomach as Hunter took my glass. He returned to pull me up to standing. His fingers worked over my buttons quickly, opening my sweater before discarding it. He pulled my tank top over my head and paused at my see-through, lacy black bra. His palms slid down my chest and over the swell of my breasts. With both of us breathing faster, he skipped down to my jeans, ripping open the button and pushing down the zipper in quick movements. He bent down in front of me as he worked them to the floor. I stepped out, only to have my leg directed to a wider stance. He hooked a finger into my panties and pulled them to the side.

I moaned, my head falling back, as a wet tongue probed my lips before circling the top of my slit. He sucked me in, making my knees go week.

"Every time I see you I want you," he said, rubbing eager fingers along my wetness. A finger worked into me as his thumb circled my clit lazily. His mouth took over for his thumb again.

"Or maybe we could just hang out in here until dinner," I said as my eyes fluttered closed and my body wound tighter.

He took one last, long suck before backing off and pulling my panties down to my ankles. Cold air brushed my aching wetness. My bra fell away a moment later.

"We'll have all night in bed, Livy. Let's spend the evening elsewhere. I'm sorry we have to be confined—I should've known what I was likely to come home to. That's something I'll need to change."

He draped the robe over my shoulders as he quickly stripped out of his shirt. I ran my hand up his perfectly sculpted chest while he worked at the buttons on his pants. He shrugged into his robe and gestured me out of the room. We walked down the stairs and toward the back of the house, hearing a murmur of voices coming from the living room. He let me out through the back door and to a covered gazebo. He flicked a switch, and soft lights lit up a hot tub and illuminated a pool beyond. With economic movements, he took the cover off the large, circular tub.

He turned to me, taking off my robe and hanging it

on a hook in the gazebo before removing his. I sighed as I sat into the hot waters. He stepped in a moment later, on the opposite side of the tub. His gaze held mine. "I wanted to talk to you about…our situation."

I put my arms along the side of the hot tub. "Okay."

"I can't share you, Olivia. If you can't be with me solely, you need to say that now before we get any more serious."

I didn't even have to think about my response. "I only want to be with you."

"Good." The edge to his voice eased somewhat. His muscles visibly relaxed. He leaned back. "I have a strange setup, but I've always only been with one woman at a time."

"Yet…you don't ask that that one woman be monogamous."

"How could I? I only…sexually engaged with a normal admin once a week or so, and for a short period of time. I gave no other part of myself. Everything I've done with you has been…abnormal. I've opened myself to you in ways I've only done once before. I couldn't ask a woman to give me more than I was willing to give to her. That's not what that contract is for."

My heart surged, warmed with his admission. "So…then…you're willing to give me more?"

"C'mere, Livy." He reached out through the waters. I took his hand, allowing him to pull me closer. He sat me in his lap and circled me with his arms. "I'm willing to give you all. I've tried to deny you, and you worked closer anyway. What's the point in resisting? You'd just steal my heart in the end anyway."

I put my face close to his, feeling the fire of love and passion lick the inside of me.

"I've never been with Blaire, so you know," he said quietly. He turned his face so his lips glanced off mine. "I've never intended to. She knew that going in."

"She's obviously pretty sexual, and I bet she's really pretty—isn't she hard to resist sometimes?"

"Not at all. No one has ever been hard to resist, past my sexual awakening. Until now. There is only one like you, Livy. Every man that sees you notices it. I'm lucky enough to have you."

"Behind all that rudeness is *this* guy. It's amazing." I shifted until I was straddling him. I fell into his kiss, passionate but soft. Deep and heartfelt.

I was falling in love. This conversation clinched it. I didn't ever want this to end.

"Do you want kids, Livy?" he murmured.

I snaked my arms around his neck. "Someday, yes."

"How many?" His hands came around my back and pulled me tighter to his chest.

I slid my cheek against his. "I don't know—two or three, depending on how early I start."

His fingers traced the skin on my back. "I never thought I'd have kids. Not since Denise. I've wanted them, though."

"It's odd for a guy to go that baby crazy," I mused aloud. Then, realizing how that sounded, I pulled back so I could look down into his deep brown eyes. "Not saying that's a bad thing—I just didn't think teenage boys, all hopped up on hormones, would be that excited about being tied down."

Hunter's big shoulders shrugged under my palms. "I wasn't at first, but I grew up as an only child. My father was a hound. My mother couldn't stand the sight of him after a while. I thought a family I created with a woman I loved, and who I thought loved me, would make me feel normal." He pulled me closer again. "I was seventeen, Olivia. My head wasn't on straight."

"But you've never stopped wanting it."

"I've never stopped wanting normal, no. But the more I've chased it, the further away it seems to get. Look at me. For years now I've enforced an employee contract that granted morally corrupt privileges. I should've been sued many times over. Instead, it's a highly sought after position. I have a fiancée I don't like, but who I agreed to so my father would walk away from my life. She tied together two businesses that had nothing to do with me. My father is still very much in my life, like it or not, and the businesses no longer have a relationship. Yet still I'm tied. I'm a workaholic because I have nothing else in my life.

"I'm so far removed from normal I don't even know the way back. Except through you. You are everything I've always wanted to be, including poor after college and looking for a job. And within you is the potential for me to achieve my dreams. You, as a person, by yourself, are perfect. You are a rare and priceless gem that I would chase to the ends of the world just to be near. Just to hope some of your effulgence rubbed off on me. I am incredibly lucky you chose me."

I kissed Hunter, clinging to him. "You are living in opposite land." I laughed through my emotion. "And incredibly sweet."

"I'm not sweet, I'm truthful. It gets me in trouble often."

"Not with me."

"Mr. Carlisle?" we heard from the back door.

"Yes, Mrs. Foster," Hunter called.

"Dinner is fifteen minutes out, and the dinning room is set for you. Miss Englewood is...elsewhere. You should be undisturbed."

"Thank you, Mrs. Foster, we'll be in shortly."

"I meant to ask you," I said to Hunter as we got out of the hot tub, "when do you find time to work out?"

"Out of everything, that is your burning question?" Hunter held out my robe. "I use the company gym, mostly, and if I don't get a chance, I use the one here. It's next to the garage."

"Ah."

He steered me inside and up to his room. Instead of letting me change into my clothes from the day, though, he handed me a pair of men's pajama bottoms and one of his T-shirts. He donned his own pair before wrapping me in his arms for a moment before we headed downstairs. "I'll get you some pajamas to wear."

"I have some at my house."

"Your bed is too small. It's made for elves."

"In *Lord of the Rings*, Elves are tall, I think. And I meant I can bring them here. I'm not sure if you realize this, but you don't have to buy an entire wardrobe for each residence. I thought I'd point that out to you. You know, as the voice of *normal*."

He kissed me on the forehead before leading me downstairs and to the dining room. The long table was set up with two places facing each other at one end. Lit candles flickered, and the light from the crystal chandelier above put off a dim glow.

I sat down to a place set with pricy china dinnerware and real silver utensils. While wearing Hunter's pajamas.

"No, you don't do normal all that well." I laughed as Mrs. Foster entered with a serving tray loaded with savory pot roast glistening in delicious-looking gravy. Potatoes and peas were already on the table in their own serving bowls, with a salad off to the side.

"She usually just makes me a plate," Hunter said as Mrs. Foster situated the beef.

"You have a pretty guest, Mr. Carlisle. I couldn't have you eating like a squatter, now could I? What would she think of me!" Mrs. Foster pursed her lips as she turned to me from her position at the head of the table. The chair had been removed to the corner, and serving spoons and forks were lined up for her use. "Now, young lady, would you like some salad?"

"Yes, please," I answered dutifully.

"And she has manners. What a nice change in this house!" Mrs. Foster took a small plate and loaded me up with salad. Without asking, she took Hunter's plate and did the same.

After agreeing to the other elements to the dish, Mrs. Foster made up a larger plate with way too much food then left the room to give us some privacy.

"She must work late hours," I said as I cut into the roast.

"Not generally. She usually leaves my plate in a warming tray."

"And she just cooks. That's it?"

"She cleans, as well. She looks after me, for the most part, so she sees to my laundry or dry cleaning, makes breakfast and dinner, and whatever I need. Blaire has her own staff."

"Must be nice," I muttered, closing my eyes as the delicious meat melted in my mouth. "Very nice. She's a great cook."

"Yes. I'm well fed." A moment later, he said, "Bruce asked about you on Friday. I told him you were seeking other employment. He'll be calling you with a job offer, I have no doubt."

I opened my mouth to tell him that Bruce already had. He was expecting an answer any day. And while I hadn't officially decided, if I was really, truly honest with myself, I still longed to say yes. The idea of doing something I loved, of following my dream, called to me. Why wouldn't it—that was the path to happiness, after all. But as happy as I would be doing that, I'd be happier with Hunter. I'd do something I hated to be close to him, and my situation wasn't even remotely that bad.

So instead, I played dumb. "A job offer? He's selling his company!"

Hunter smirked. "He's gotten a taste for business now—he's already thinking of the prospects for his computer games."

"Oh. The hobby. I doubt his wife will be pleased."

"Are wives ever pleased?" Hunter's eyes glittered in the soft light. A smile tickled his lips, boosting his handsomeness.

After a moment, his mirth turned into a furrowed brow. I was still staring.

"You're handsome," I said in answer to his unspoken question. "I can't help but look."

"Ditto," he responded with that hot smirk of his. His gaze started a slow burn as he lifted a potato to his full lips. In his eyes held a promise, and I was eager to feel him deliver it.

Chapter 14

———❧———

HUNTER CLOSED THE door to his bedroom behind him. We'd sat at dinner for a while, eating and chatting, before Mrs. Foster bustled in with cheesecake. I'd tried not to eat too much, knowing that I'd be getting intimate with Hunter soon after, but everything tasted so *good*! I couldn't help myself.

I was surprised at how easy it was to talk to Hunter. Being that he was a man of few words at work, a trait that had carried over into lunches and plane rides, I hadn't expected him to open up so much. As we spoke, though, his sense of humor showed itself in the form of sarcasm, and his ideas and observations enhanced whatever silly thing I threw at him. It was quite possibly the most relaxed and easy I had ever seen him.

"Do you want to watch TV?" he asked as he hovered by the light switch.

I crawled up onto the bed, needing to lie down after that feast. "Which side do you want me?"

"The side furthest from the door. If a burglar comes

in, I'll die first."

I snorted. "Well thought out."

"TV?" he asked again.

"Or…just bed and fondling?"

The light clicked off, plunging the room into darkness. I saw Hunter's body move across the room, black against very dark gray. A dim light switched on near the bathroom, showering the bed in a soft glow.

"Put candles on your list of to-buys," I said.

"Noted." He stripped out of his clothes. I marveled at his body, tracing his muscles with my gaze as he moved and shifted. He slid into the covers and scooted up to my body. He tugged my shirt over my head before reaching low to strip me of the pajama bottoms. His hand traveled up my skin, leaving a warm trail in its wake, before cupping a breast. His lips connected with mine, light and sweet. He traced my bottom lip with his tongue while pinching a nipple. Shooting pleasure coursed down to my core.

"Do we need to use protection?" he asked as his hand drifted between my legs. His fingers ran between my swollen sex. I spread my legs, giving him more access.

"We've been fine without it so far."

"Will you miss a pill? I should've asked if we needed to stop by your house first."

"Oh. No, I haven't gotten out of the habit of carrying them in my purse. In college, you never knew where you might end up." I felt his fingers stall for a brief moment. "No, not like that! I mean, sometimes like that—I did have boyfriends. But sometimes I would spend the night at Kimberly's if we were at a party closer to her house. Or a different friend. Very rarely boys. I wasn't that exciting."

"You're plenty exciting."

I ran my hands over his shoulders before curling them around his neck and bringing his head closer. Hunter plunged two fingers in, getting me nice and slick, before trailing his lips down my chest and sucking in a nipple.

"Hmm," I said, running my fingers through his hair.

He switched sides as his fingers sped up, his thumb working my nub while his fingers hit the right areas. I arched, applying pressure to the top of his shoulders, needing his mouth on me. Wanting him to finish what he'd started earlier in the night.

He moved that way immediately, pulling back the cover so the light fell on my nude body. His tongue licked up my center before his mouth sucked at the top. His fingers continued to work as his tongue made circles around my clit before then manipulating it from side to side.

"Yes!" I rocked my hips up into his mouth. I arched again, losing control. My hands moved across the mattress and up to my hair, clutching in fistfuls as the pleasure tightened my core. "Oh holy—" I arched and then gyrated, writhing. His mouth was ecstasy, sucking and manipulating, as his fingers worked, rubbing just right.

"Oh yes, Hu—yes. Oh. Oh yes." I arched again like a woman possessed, squeezing my eyes shut against the tumult. "Almost…almost…"

A climax blasted my body apart, having me yank my own hair as the sweet feeling of orgasm soaked up every fiber of my being. "Ohh, that was good." I melted into the mattress as his tongue made lazy circles around my sex.

He kissed up my body, each touch of his lips giving me a delightful shiver. When he got to my mouth, I pushed him to his back. *My turn.*

I climbed on top of him, threading my thigh between his legs so his rock-hard erection was against skin without hope of finding my opening. That would come later.

I started at his mouth, giving him teasing, light kisses. When he lifted his head, wanting more, I backed off with a smile. His hands slid up my back, trying to capture me. Instead, I grabbed him by the wrists and pushed them above his head.

"Have you ever been tied up?" I asked, licking across his full bottom lip.

"Usually I would ask that of a woman."

"Have you?"

"No." Lust infused his voice.

I trailed those teasing kisses down his chin and back, starting to slide down his body slowly. "Something to explore."

"Or blindfolded."

I could hear the excitement in his voice. He obvious-ly knew I'd use those items to take my time and have my way with him. Not many men would say no to that.

I certainly wouldn't.

I circled his nipple with my tongue before sucking it in. I bit lightly, enhancing the feeling. He sucked in a breath before groaning. I switched to the other side, doing the same, before running my tongue down his defined six-pack. I kissed each muscle before running my hands back and forth over him, loving the feeling of a hard, cut man.

I slid lower, lifting my body and adjusting my posi-tioning so the tip of his manhood would slide across my taut, sensitive nipple.

We both moaned.

I stayed there a moment, rubbing back and forth on him, feeling my sex swell even more, and seeing his hips start to lightly thrust upward.

"Do you have any lube?" I asked, still playing with that tip.

He reached to his nightstand, making me get up so he could get into the drawer. He bought out a tube of lube. No frills, no taste, just something to get the job done.

It was clearly for his alone time.

I spread the cold gel over my breasts before tossing it to the side and working my body between his legs. I wrapped my breasts around his cock. Slowly, I moved up and down, stroking him.

I looked up, watching him watch his tip emerge from my breasts, before being swallowed again.

"Maybe no to the blindfold," he said in a thick voice.

I smiled, working a little faster. I knew I could take him all the way right here. His hands fisted in the sheets. His body strained. Those beautiful pecs turned into mountains.

But I wanted to deep-throat. That would be way more impressive than what I was doing. I hoped.

I tilted my head down, trying not to make it look as awkward as it felt, and pushed down so his tip popped out—right into my awaiting mouth.

"Oooohhhh, Livy," he gasped. His body went rigid.

Jackpot.

I worked him faster, stroking him with my breasts until I could get him into my mouth, and then sucking hard. His head fell into the pillow.

"Faster," he breathed.

As awkward as it was, I increased the pace, squeezing him as tightly as I could and sucking as much as I could. I bounced over him, feeling his wild thrusts into me. He was too wild, though. Too desperate. He wasn't getting enough from this setup.

In a quick decision, I let go of my breasts and sucked him in as far as I could. His tip hit the back of my throat.

"Oh!" Hunter said in a surprised release of breath.

I backed off quickly and immediately sucked him in deep again, stroking with one hand and cupping his balls with the other. I massaged, stroked and sucked, as fast as I could, feeling that smooth skin enter and leave my mouth.

"Livy—"

That was all the warning I got. He gave a long groan, shaking on the bed as an orgasm stole his speech. As he calmed, I couldn't help myself. I had to break the mood.

"I'll just run to the bathroom really quick," I said as I climbed off the bed.

"Mouthwash is in the cabinet on the right, if that's what you're looking for."

It was exactly what I was looking for. I hastened into the large bathroom with double sinks, his toiletries around one, the other bare, and searched the cabinet. I found the green bottle immediately and took a swig before heading back out to the peacefully resting man molded from the gods.

I crawled up next to him and put my head in the indent of his shoulder. He looped his arm around me and hugged me close.

"I would love to do more, but I am also so extremely relaxed," he said, and sighed. "Give me a minute to recover."

"I'll just do the work until you're ready to join in," I said, rising up and throwing a leg over his groin.

"It's been so long since I let a woman lead. I forgot how pleasant it is to be a sloth while still reaping the rewards." His smile made me blink in a daze for a second. The man was so incredibly handsome.

I laid my body on top of him and kissed those soft lips. His arms came around me as he kissed me back. I reached under me to grab his softened phallus. Gently I stroked, feeling life surge into it quickly. I smiled over his lips.

"You have the magic touch," he said, probably in response to my smile.

I shifted my body so his growing erection fit against my wetness. I moved along his shaft, closing my eyes with the small points of pleasure firing into me. My breath sped up as he hardened further. His hands gripped my hips as I stroked with my body.

Rising to the top, I tilted my hips, and then slowly slid back down. His girth filled me, making me moan as heat worked up from point of contact.

"God you feel good," Hunter whispered, eyes closed. His fingers gripped my skin tightly.

I rocked forward as I dropped my hand between my spread legs. I manipulated my pleasure center as I moved him in and out with gyrating hips. Pleasure multiplied exponentially. Immediately.

"Hmm." I licked my lips and worked myself faster. The outside sensations merged with the feeling of him moving inside me.

I felt his palm against my sensitive nipple. I gasped, sitting down harder than I intended. Stabs of ecstasy pierced me. My breathing turned into panting. My movements became less fluid and more hectic. I rocked over him, strumming with my fingers and leaning into his treatment of my nipple. "Yes, Hunter—yes. Yes, baby." I rocked and sat, rocked and sat. My fingers worked. So did his.

Something tore loose. My control fled. Pleasure took over.

Pulling my feet under me, I rose up and sat even harder, taking him all the way in with hard, rough movements. He groaned, his hand starting to shake on my breast. My fingers worked faster. My body rose and sat, harder and harder. The bed started to rock. Then squeak. Wood groaned. Still I worked harder, the sensations starting to become unbearable.

"Almost, Hunter," I said in between rough panting. "Almost there."

My pants turned into moaning grunts. My body tightened. My muscles followed.

"Almost—" I clenched my teeth, needing a final push. Needing something to send me over the edge.

"Come, baby," Hunter commanded urgently.

Like a release valve, it all came crashing down. Wave after ruthless wave of body-shaking climax hit me. I half yelled, half moaned from it, going completely rigid. I had no idea if he came with me.

I did not care.

The climax tore through me, never ending. It felt so damn good.

When the last of the quakes drained away, I fell on top of him. My limbs splashed around his body. My head rested in the hollow between his neck and shoulder.

"Did you orgasm?" I asked in a sleepy voice. Because I would roll over and play dead if not. He'd have to do all the work to finish up. I didn't even want to lift my head.

"Yes, baby," he whispered in a tired voice. He held me tight. I felt his heart beating against mine. "Thank you, Livy, for putting up with me. For opening me up and forcing me to feel again. I want to do this right with you. I want to try and give you the man you deserve. Regardless of all else, I want to give you a real relationship. I want to try and make it work."

My heart warmed and my lips curved into a smile. He was facing his fears and trying to use his heart again. With me. I'd been given a crack and I'd wormed my way in. All I had to do now was hold on and let what was between us grow.

I kissed him, deep and heartfelt, giving my answer physically. I wanted to try, too, because I knew he was capable of deep and profound love, and I wanted him to find that again.

With me.

I sighed in contentment and fell into a deep, comfortable sleep.

If only every day could end like this one. It would make everything else in life bearable.

The End

The story continues in the third book:

More, *Please*

"GOOD MORNING, BEAUTIFUL."

My eyes fluttered open as dim sunlight streamed in through the windows. The air had that "early morning smell" that said it was way too early to have my eyes open.

Hunter stood by my bed holding a tray with legs. I could just make out a small white vase with a flower, and the rim of a glass. The smell of bacon wafted toward me.

"Hi." I rubbed my eyes, trying to get the sleep out. "What time is it?"

"It's five thirty. I need to drop you off at home on my way into the office."

"Why do you go to work so early?" I coughed, trying to wake up my vocal cords.

"I'm hoping I can actually concentrate today. I need to get some things ironed out for this takeover. Here, Mrs. Foster made you breakfast."

In another situation I might've whined about getting up, and then stayed securely under the covers for another fifteen minutes, but with a tray of breakfast being presented to me I wasn't about to complain. I scooted up and braced the pillows behind me, suddenly wide awake. "She must work really long hours."

Hunter's grin left me star-struck for a moment, as I took in his handsomeness. It was almost as pleasant seeing him first thing in the morning as having breakfast delivered.

"She must like when I entertain, which was why the late night, but she's usually here early."

Hunter put the tray over my lap and laid one of his shirts next to it. Then he leaned over and gently touched his lips to mine. As he was about to back away, he must have decided better of it, and connected a little more firmly. His hand touched the back of my head as he nibbled my lips, moaning softly. When he stood up, a small smile touched his lips again. "*That* I have never had." He brushed my hair back from my face. "A woman to wake up to."

He gazed at me with soft brown eyes for a moment longer. With another small smile, he gestured to my tray and turned to walk away. "Eat. It's getting cold."

I didn't have to be told twice.

As I ate, I reflected on my luck to have ended up in Hunter Carlisle's bed. Yes, he had problems, and some serious baggage in the form of a contractually obligated fiancée, but he was trying to open up. He'd admitted last night that he wanted to try and have a relationship.

I was all for it. Right after I ate breakfast.

A half-hour later I sat back and looked out the window, and finally decided I should get up. I'd thought

Hunter would be encouraging me to get moving, but he'd gone downstairs shortly after delivering breakfast and hadn't returned. I figured I should be a big girl before he got irritated and said I couldn't come back.

I glanced at my pile of clothes, and then at his pajama bottoms and shirt. I should wear one set, but I wanted to wear the other. As it was my first time over here, and I really wanted to come back, I reached for my own clothes. Testing the boundaries would have to wait until next time.

I shrugged into my jeans, a pleasant soreness from last night acting as a reminder, and walked a few steps to glance in the mirror.

I flinched.

I had black smudges under my eyes, my hair looked like I'd stuck my finger in an electric socket, and one side of my face still had a light dusting of blush.

"After seeing this face, he'll rethink wanting normal." I cleaned myself up as best I could, using the tried and tested method of licking the pad of my finger and wiping it under my eye to remove the black. I tied my hair back and picked up my handbag.

All was quiet outside Hunter's room. I made my way downstairs, too shy to call out, as we weren't the only ones there. I didn't want to alert the fiancée to my whereabouts. He wasn't in the living room, nor in the dining room. I popped my head in the kitchen and found Mrs. Foster wiping down the counters.

"Have you seen Hunter?" I asked in a tiny voice.

She glanced up with raised eyebrows. "Oh. Good morning. Yes, he's in the library."

"Great, thanks." I turned to leave before remembering my manners. I turned back. "And thanks for breakfast. It was delicious."

"No problem, sweetie. That's my job." She smiled at me before returning to her task.

I should've probably brought down the empty tray. *Oops.*

I headed off toward the area of the house I hadn't seen to yet. I figured that was where I would find the library. As I got halfway down the hall, I heard voices raised in an argument. I slowed down.

"Blaire, I gave permission for visitors of a sexual nature—I did *not* give permission for sex parties. You can spend your time how you will, but in my house, there will be boundaries."

"Oh, really?" a girlie voice spat back at what was definitely Hunter. "As I recall, you didn't specify any of this in your precious *contract.*"

"If you look at the detail, you will see that I covered any acts that might reflect badly on my dealings in a social or business aspect. My housemate having wild orgies, participating in flogging, bondage, self-mutilation, among other things, is not something I want your strangers spreading around my circles of influence."

"Your live-in *housemate?* You arrogant prick! What happened to *fiancée?*"

"This is a business arrangement, Blaire, between your

father and mine. I went along with it to attempt to cut my father out of my life. This was understood in the negotiations that you sat in on. Since he has *not* been cut out of my life—he's more in it now than before this agreement—I'll be looking into a breach of contract."

"Is that right?" she snapped with a cutting and snide voice. "So let me get this straight. You won't fuck me, but you don't want anyone else fucking me, either? What am I supposed to do, take up a monk robe?"

I heard a sigh that was distinctly Hunter's. "I'm not saying to stop having sex, Blaire. I'm saying go about it with some discretion, or take it somewhere else."

"Somewhere else? I live here, too, *Mister* Carlisle. And don't think I don't know what's going on here. Your cook told me all about your pretty little piece of ass. She was trying to throw it in my face, the bitch. I'll bet that's the street trash secretary I've heard about, right? You're not only fucking the hired help, now you're bringing them around?"

I withered against the wall. I should really turn around and walk away. I didn't need to hear any of this. At the same time, the roadblock that was Blaire, and the contract she represented, was now very clear. She might not love Hunter, but she wanted him. She didn't sound like a girl that was happy not getting what she wanted.

"Watch yourself there, Blaire," Hunter was saying in a low and dangerous tone.

Blaire scoffed. "So it is her. That's your type, is it? Sweet and naive. I should've known. Men like you don't want sexually enlightened; you want the dumb little virgin that you can lead around by the nose. Well *fuck you*, Hunter Carlisle. If I can't have any fun, neither will you. If you keep bringing her around, I'll make your life hell, you got that? I'll show up at your business lunches, I'll spread nasty rumors around your social circle—if you try to trade me in for a troll like that, so help me God, you will rue the day!"

A beat of silence passed before Hunter said, "Are you done?"

"Not even remotely, you controlling piece of shit. Not even remotely." I heard the pounding of bare feet on wood before a wild-eyed woman emerged from the room along the hall. I sucked in a breath at her beauty. Hunter might've called it manufactured, but everyone else would call it model-worthy. Long blond hair framed her heart-shaped face in a series of waves. Her full lips, colored deep red, were currently pressed tight. Bright blue eyes and high cheekbones made her stunning. A long silk robe parted at the front, revealing a slim body with large, perky breasts and a cleanly shaved pubic area. She'd been fighting virtually in the nude. It hadn't slowed her down at all.

"Well, well, well. What have we here?" She slowed in her sensuous walk, not bothering to pull her robe closed. "If it isn't our deflowered little princess…"

I stayed frozen against the wall for a moment, terrified for reasons I couldn't explain.

"Come to find your master?" She stopped in front of

me. Her hip jutted out.

I tore my eyes away from her bald pubic area, and then her exposed breasts. I really wasn't used to being confronted by naked people.

"Excuse me," I said, trying to slide along the wall like a coward, trying to sneak past. Her eyes shone with a maniacal flare that said she was capable of extremely damaging things. I didn't think rules bothered her, and I knew I would be the target if she decided to torch someone's house while that someone was tied up inside.

"What's sad is, you think he actually likes you. Let me fill you in, sweetheart. Hunter Carlisle doesn't like anyone but himself. He is a selfish bastard with a giant ego, and he wants a fixer-upper to drape across his arm to appear like one of the *people*. To seem like one of his workers. You're Cinderella for now, but you'll be old news tossed in the garbage when he has what he wants."

"Blaire!" Hunter's voice boomed through the hallway. I jumped.

A vicious smile spread across Blaire's face as she beheld me. "Watch your back—I may decide to stick a knife in it. I would hate it to be a surprise."

She took a small canister out of the pocket of her robe and unscrewed the top. Turning toward Hunter, she poured a little line of white powder onto the skin between her thumb and forefinger. She threw Hunter a malicious glare before bending her head down and snorting up the line. She wiped her nose with her thumb before screwing the top back on the canister. She smirked. "Oops. Another rule broken."

With a last scathing look at me, she turned and sauntered away.

"I'm sorry about that," Hunter said in a troubled voice. "She's never been one to maneuver, but I'm starting to think her father was offloading her, rather than securing her a comfortable future."

"She's...precious." I tucked a flyaway behind my ear and leaned against the wall. "And she's always here?"

Hunter's gaze turned to me. He closed the distance between us and wrapped his arms around me, pulling me into his body. "Yes, unfortunately. She doesn't work, and she doesn't have a place of her own. Part of the deal was that she'd move out of her father's house and live with me. I think she thought I'd buckle and become a husband, of sorts. One like my father was. I've disappointed her."

"Then why doesn't she want to find someone else?"

"Money." Hunter kissed the crown of my head.

"So...you're locked in?" I couldn't prevent the hollowness in my voice.

Hunter squeezed me tighter. "I'll figure something out."

As Hunter led me to the library, my mind started whirling. He might be able to figure something out, but if that woman didn't get what she wanted, I'd be the first she'd blame.

I remembered the vicious, manic look to her eye and shivered. It was a pretty safe bet that she was capable of terrible, malicious acts. If Hunter brought me here again, she'd probably find ways to make trouble. I'd made a terrible enemy, one likely to be as unpredictable as she was dangerous.

Cold hands of fear crept through my body. I'd have to be on my guard, but would that be enough?

.

29298221R00125

Made in the USA
Middletown, DE
13 February 2016